DIVA'S REVENGE

Brandee Foxxx Kassadine

Copyright page

Printed in

The United States of America

Back from Broken

©Copyright 2021

ISBN: **979-8-9852437-0-3**

Written by Brandee Foxxx Kassadine

Table of Contents

Contents

Dedication

Dedication... I would like to dedicate this book to my heroes...

Before I knew what strong was all these women showed me, when I had no love for myself, they loved me in their own fearless way and always encouraged me to be the best...

I love you to the moon and back...

Viola Harris,

Constance Harris,

 Johnnie Kathy King,

Zaneka Chapman,

Sassy O'Hara

But the best love and grace has been from God...

Prologue

"Mama you know I love my fruity pebbles. Where are they?" Said Tanesha.

"Where they always are, the cereal aisle!" Mama Vi said.

"Okay let me grab those and some hot pockets, and I'll be ready to go!" said Tanesha.

"Okay Hun!" In the back of Tanesha mind, she had to be very careful when being in public places with Mama Vi. Reason being is anyone could spot her, and make matters hard. Mama Vi is forever stuck in her ways, and refuses to let me grow up into a woman.

As Tanesha is walking through the store, she sees a face that is familiar. She has been through this a million times seeing guys from "The block" out, and about. So, she would do what she always did and, ignore them or hurry up and disappear. Her night time career is sometimes too much for her, but hey it pays the bills.

Meanwhile...

"Hey Jamaica fool we need to hurry up, and go fool" says J-Money.

"Yeah, you know how long it's going to take to get to the Nawf, and we got to stop by the spot for some shit!" echoed RayRay.

"Nigga I know, I just want all to see this yella bone bitch that I been smashing from up the street!" said Jamaica,

"Nigga if that ho looks like Crystal, I'm go roast you and her, cause Crystal may can suck a mean dick, but that ho was out of there!" yelled New Jack before laughing with the other guys.

"Nigga whatever, all done banged some ugly Hos. Especially you RayRay. That's your specialty."

"Nigga all my hos be loyal though. They go fuck good and hold a nigga down. Believe that."

"Aright nigga, shut the fuck up, here she is with her T-Lady."

Meanwhile...

Tanesha: "Chile why is yo face looking all crazy and shit. I told you I was almost done?" Mama Vi said looking at Tanesha who had alarm on her face.

"Nothing I think I have gas that's all."

" Umm hum, whatever go get me some..."

Meanwhile...

"Aye Tanesha what's good?" Jamaica says as him and the others approach Tanesha.

"Uh hi Jamaica" Tanesha fumbles.

Diva's Revenge

"Dayum Jamaica you might redeem yourself from Crystal with this one." says RayRay

"Mamas do you have any friends like you or your sisters?" New Jack smiling asks.

"No just me sweetie"

"How the fuck you run into this lame ass nigga, what you were depressed or some shit?" joked New Jack.

"Jamaica is sweet and we been kicking it for a while." "On purpose" J-Money demanded to know.

"Well with my crazy work schedule I only see him some nights. He works a lot to so we kind of meet in the middle." Says Tanesha

RayRay and J-Money give each other curious looks. Before Tanesha is able to say bye and move along before the matter blew up, and shit hit the fan.

"Boy you rushing me to go but as soon as I turn my back you chasing these knuckle head ass boys." Screamed Mama Vi. She shoved the basket into Tanesha who was both scared and stunned of what was about to happen. Now RayRay and J-Money was looking at each other.

"Baby which one of all here is tryna court my son?" smiling Mama Vi asked.

No one replied. She looked at Tanesha who stood there almost in tears. Mama Vi didn't know what all the strange looks were for but she knew with Tanesha that was bound to happen. All four of the boys looked at each other and the three walked off leaving Jamaica there standing. Tanesha just stood there with plea in her eyes shaking her head. Jamaica eyes narrowed to slits as he too shook his head out of disgust and walked away.

3 days later...

"Police are saying that Brian Taylor aka Tanesha Duvall was found in a dumpster on Lancaster Rd. Police are speculating about time of death. Brian was a prostitute in the Cedar Springs/Oaklawn part of town. Police are leaning towards foul play while prostituting and are closing the case. No witnesses or evidence has come forth in the case. If you have any info in this case.... "

Mama Vi slammed the remote down as she sat in her living room and cried for what seemed like the millionth time since she got the news. She looks out her window and watch as people in her neighborhood go about their business as if nothing has happened when everyone knows the truth. She keeps checking her watch in anticipation of Tanesha four friends to finally get here. She hasn't made up in her mind how to tell them what she knows but she knows that they deserve the truth...

Diva's Revenge

"Sit down babies. What I'm about to tell you is going to be hard to understand. It may change a lot of the way you are about to view the world, but you as Tanesha's friends are entitled to know. I know that you have been watching the news about Tanesha? It's not all true. Everyone in the hood knows that Jamaica and his boys killed her. Why, I really haven't been able to wrap my head around it but we all know how wild Tanesha was. She was my baby and I love her more than life itself but I know Tanesha was not killed the way these bitches are saying. God has my son now and he is safe from all things that would wish harm to him. Here is some stuff I feel you guys would love to have from my baby and I want all to be the best in life like Tanesha always wanted all to be. I love y'all and know that you are always welcome here..."

The four of them sat Indian style on Mama Vi's floor and went through the box of stuff. It was a bunch of mixed emotions as they sat there. Some sad, some happy at old pictures of Tanesha and them. By them all being in middle school, it was limited to how much time they were allowed to spend with her. As the tears and hours rolled by, the four of them all came to one conclusion that day. No matter what it took, they would honor Tanesha and show their love for her.

PART I
10 YEARS LATER...

Chapter 1

My name is Mocha Simone and most bitches feel threatened by me because I possess something that a lot of hos don't. I exude sex appeal no matter what and I am alluring to most men with a working dick. I stand 5'08 and I have 36C breast and 38 hips. No waist line and I am a boss bitch. I drive the nicest cars and live in Desoto. Most blacks in Dallas all move here when they get their shit together as a sign of upgrading. At 24 I am doing nicely but with the help of my three girls, I feel our time and planning is about to pay off.

I have my good days and I have my bad ones where I really don't have much energy. I keep going, I am a prostitute and because I have been at it so long, I have become what you called "seasoned." I work when I feel like it and deal with who I want to deal with. Because of my well-kept maintenance on myself I have been blessed to have met some top-notch clients. But now all of that has changed since I met J-Money.

J-Money is a dope nigga from the hood I grew up in. He thinks that we just met but we've been knowing each other. He is ten years older than me. When I was a youngster in the hood he never paid me any mind, but now we have dealings and they are explosive. It all started when I copped a cheap ass Crown Victoria car to pose as a stripper. I came to his weed spot and got weed from him. Gradually, I started to blow a blunt or two with him. He would ask me where I strip at so him and his boys can come see me. I blew him off from that because I wanted to limit my contact with others until we were ready for the next phase.

I also have to dodge this grimy bitch Dior and her crew cause all of them are messy. I use to cop shit from them when I was low budget. They get all the knock off shit. Since Tasha upgraded me and my girls game, I wouldn't be caught dead in they shit. But a bitch had to do something right? J-Money is cool and we text and shit all the time. I only see him when I buy weed. But I feel it's about time for us to take things to the next level I have gave him some head in the car a couple of times just to test the waters but from his conversation he wants a bitch to be more than that and it falls in line exactly with what Scoop told us about him. He loves a freaky bitch that has a head on her shoulders. Oh J-Money do I ever. He talks to me all the time about his crew and how he feels and I absorb it all and take it back to my girls.

Knowledge is sometimes more powerful than money. When I come around him I have to wear really wild outfits cause by him being a major nigga he would recognize a lot of shit. He fucks with this lame ho name Connie and has a couple of baby Mamas but none of them knew what it took to keep him. I gave him just enough to want more. It's really taxing on me to drive this piece of shit car because I haven't rolled in nothing this crappy since high school but hey we all got our mission. The other thing about J money that I have to contend with is this nigga is super paranoid and he always suspect something, or someone out to get him.

This is why he only lets me give him head. He feels for holes poked in condoms to try to trap him. He acts weird about pulling money out in front of me and he does little crazy test to see if I am one of those grimy hoes to try to get over on him. Like one time he purposely dropped some money and drugs in front of me to see if I would pick it up. He never lets me see him unlock his phone.

I laugh at the thought cause if this nigga only knew the bitch sitting in front of him was the truth. I wear Escada and Chanel to the grocery store. My whole house is done in Ethan Alan and Catoni designs. I drive an Audi A8 and a Range Rover. A lot of people think I resemble Kenya Moore because of my build but it varies because my weight tends to fluctuate a lot .I go get my hair done Ah-Donis shop where all the best of the best in Dallas go .You not going to sit in her chair for less than $300 .Me and my crew go weekly but in due time Mr. J money will come to see who me and my crew really are!

Diva's Revenge

J money and his crew are a hard group of niggas to get next to and me even having his number says a lot but from what Scoop has been telling us about them for years is now paying off. Me and my girls have changed our whole life to mold into who these niggas want us to be so we can teach these niggas and the hood we came from a valuable lesson. When we see each other I pretend to be pressed for time and it's him that wants to linger which is exactly what I want. I never come across as needy and never let him give me free weed .Now things are heating up because he wants to go out for the first time to do something.

I talked to Scoop and the girls and together we weighed all my options. He is paranoid so a club is out of the question. You don't want to go to somewhere too upscale cause your past could come haunt you but you have to pick someplace where you have control .I also want something where I can go to the mall out his pockets so he can think he is upgrading me. So I suggest that we go see a movie but the place is the key.

"It's not just a movie theater it's a place to dine while you watch movies." I am replaying our conversation back in my head to see if I overplayed my hand. "So what's up Ms. Mocha? When a nigga going to get to do more then serve you weed and get ate up?"

"It's on you daddy. You the one with the hectic schedule" Mocha replied in a seductive tone.

"Yeah but it's you that could be with me at night instead of sliding down a pole."

"So what you want a bitch to slow down and focus on one pole?"

"Hell yeah! See the only difference is this one not gold but what it spit is!" J money says as he lay back and smokes his blunt and grabs his dick.

"This is all of a sudden for you! What brought all this on daddy?"

"Shit it's you that's been doing all the running mamas. Look let's go slow how about we do this. You pick something for us to do." Mocha knows she can't appear too eager so she had to go through the motions of leading him to wanting what she wanted.

"Okay so what's up with the Spy Club on Wednesday" Mocha suggest. She knew this was completely out of the question.

"Fuck no! Girl you crazy! That's a death trap!" he yelled. Now Mocha had to go for somewhere that she knew he would feel they weren't ready for yet.

"OK what about Mansion on Turtle Creek?"

"Girl quit playing you ain't never even been in there." J-Money laughs and rolls his eyes .She laughs too because that's where her and the girls go every week to do spa time.

"OH, besides I wouldn't have shit to wear for there" she replied.

"Damn all you got is stripper shit? I mean I got shit for it, you know a nigga stay ready" J money boasts.

"Well that definitely kills that idea. How about Studio Movie Grill?"

"Now baby girl that might be what's up and as far as your gear goes we can take care of that, what size you wear?"

"See this why niggas should not get high on his own supply. "She states

"You never ask a woman her age or size. We need to just go to the mall huh" Mocha thought wondering which mall can she go to without being recognized. So she chose the furthest one she knew.

"OK we can go to Vista Ridge." she offered.

"Cool cool, that's what's up."

Mocha sat back and thought about the sequence of events that happened next. He was the perfect gentleman to her and they had so much fun. She took him to one of her favorite stores and went easy on him for a nice rack on her clothes. He came off of the money with no hesitation and the movie was just as nice. Score one for the home team. It was nice to ride in something she's used to. He says it's his duck off but I don't know how you can duck off in a Mercedes S550 fully loaded. If you only knew Mr. J- Money, in a matter of time that will all be mine and more. I picked up my phone as I got back in the Crown Vic and I called the girls and Scoop to give them updates of the events. We laughed but concluded that things are going smoothly.

Diva's Revenge

Chapter 2

itch I told you I would have all the new Balenciaga shit as soon as it comes out." Tasha exclaims over the phone.

"I'm the truth and it's time for me to pick up where a bitch left off. I know y'all was suffering with Dior knock off shit."

Yeah this is Tasha Kelly. I am what all these small skinny bitches should fear, I bring the noise for big girls and I'm proud of my weight. I'm the same size as Jill Scott and the old Jennifer Hudson. My face is flawless cause I wear all the right makeup .I learned from the best how to pick clothes that are for my size and colors too.

My favorite is red. I am known all over Dallas and Houston as a one of the best boosters. I make a tons of money from doing it and have built a good clientele .I just came home from a two year bid for fucking with a lame ho on a major lick at Sakk's. It fucked up my crew's masterplan and set things off by three years. Now I'm back and ready to put in my work. As soon as I came home my first two missions was to handle these hos name Dior, J-Shun and TT. They were the ultimate low budget bitches that was making it hard for me and my crew. They stole all the knockoff and discount shit and sold to all the hood rats.

My loyal clients that only cop the finest just went and bought the real until I popped back in. Dior and her crew's mouths got the best of them on this occasion 'cause they've been popping off at Ah-Donis shop. Now I feel it's time to show them who runs shit around here. It's sad because I really like TT and she has a lot of potential out of the three. J-Shun is the tallest and ugliest of them and is constantly in the ugliest clothes and drama. I give TT her props she rocks human hair and even comes through every now and then in a real Coach or Michael Kors bag .They all share a fixed up Grand Marquis and live in the hood part of Dallas called Red Bird.

They pose no threat but they must be dealt with because someone at Ah-Donis shop told me that J- Shun be in New Jack face and that is a no no. Let me explain a little about Ah-Donis beauty shop. It is right in the center of Dallas and all the baddest bitches go there.

Every THOT in Dallas goes there with the hopes of snagging a on nigga from next door at Spud's barbershop. Ah-Donis is the truth when it comes to hair and turned down the chance to be Rihanna personal stylist to stay in the hood. If it happened in the hood its go be known at Ah-Donis shop. First you must be fly when you come through 'cause Adonis is fly as fuck and all eyes are on what you are wearing, what you driving and who you fucking.

Her shop became important when Scoop told me that Spud's is where New Jack gets his hair and face done every Thursday. Everyone already knows me for coming through selling clothes so it was about being there when New Jack came with a truck full of all the things he liked to wear.

I loaded my Infiniti truck with all my things and went to Ah-Donis to begin to wait. In the process I made a few contacts with old connects and let it be known that I was back in town. I have yet to run into Dior and her crew but I know the time is coming. As I wait I listen as girls tell me stories about how flashy New Jack is and how he is the leader of his crew. I laugh at this because all the right people know that it's Jazmire man Ray Ray that is really the leader.

From the stuff that Scoop said he likes to wear, he is the flashy one of the group so I went out my way to get shit I know he won't resist. As I play on my phone and listen to the chatter, I hear a funny story about him leaving J-Shun with the check at Pappadeaux one time. Just as I'm laughing I see out the corner of my eye a midnight blue Ashton Martin pull up.

He sits in the car and finishes his business on his phone. I get up and pull down my Banana Republic high waisted skirt throw on my tweed Chanel jacket and grab my electric blue Birkin bag. As I step out the shop and prepared to enter Spud's, I see him casually raised his head to look me over. This ass got his attention for sure. Just as luck would have it he's parked next to me so as I made trips back and forth to the truck I wasn't unnoticed. He got out of his car in a pair of leather true religion pants and a thick cream Michael Bastian sweater that was all brought together with a pair of $3000 Gucci Python loafers.

He put on shades that I'm sure he would keep on while inside Spud's. As I showed a few cheaper pieces to the fellas, New Jack gave dap to a lot of niggas before he finally made his way over to where I was. His first words knocked the wind out of me.

"So this the big girl that is shutting down all the skinny bitches in Dallas? Well I agree that you bad now let's see how much of my money you about to start getting. Don't try any of that knockoff shit 'cause you go get roasted like your coworkers J-Shun and crew!" he says while flashing a million dollar smile.

"Baby I only have one coworker and she lives in Houston. Second, just make sure your pockets can match your mouth. For all I know that Ashton can be a lease or expensive rental and those could be your brother clothes. You can't be that on you wearing last year Gucci. Don't nobody wear Gucci anymore anyway but that's for another day." Tasha snapped back never missing a beat.

"And how I know that jacket ain't from TJ Maxx not Chanel?" replied New Jack.

"Cause I look like money! I could never look like shit from TJ Maxx.

"Now if you through bumping can we spend some money."

"Let me see what you got."

Over the next hour or so New Jack and I exchanged cracks on each other but $3000 later I earned his respect as a certified booster. He wanted to place orders for select shit which was fine by me cause he gave me more access.

Overtime he and his crew became major customers and I was able to stop all the shop selling I was doing. I still kept my regulars from Ah-Donis but New Jack and his crew had a lot of demands. Not only did we supply them but all the people in their lives, it was nothing for me to make ten to fifteen thousand off of them in a weekend.

As time progressed, I started to sink my claws into him. Our conversations on the phone went from "Hey fat ass is what you got for me hidden between them thighs?"

"Miss sexy mama what you gonna put your daddy in that's go set me apart from these lame cats?"

At first our meetings was always at Spud's or on the block around a lot of people but now we meet alone. Often he spends more time just kicking it with me .I even get a text from him asking what I'm doing .This is exciting to the crew 'cause he is known as a tramp or in my circle we call niggas and hos that have a lot of sex partners crunchy. I'm not trying to stop him from doing his thing I just want a few seconds of his time to get in close. I know I won't ever be the only one but I intend to be the only one close to him. You feel me?

I started to purposely show him and his crew love. I would charge them next to nothing for top notch shit. We started to flirt more heavily and in doing so our talks got more deep. But what I found out about New Jack is that we share a level of sexual openness that Scoop couldn't know.

New Jack is an exhibitionist and he loves oral sex. I love to perform it and gets a thrill out of me giving him head while driving or in places where people can see. He also loves for his toes to be sucked and his salad to be tossed. I don't mind because in our talks he told me that something a lot of women don't do or don't do good. For a big bitch I am flexible and long winded. So we have fun exploring each other. He's obsessed with it and calls and texts me all the time to tell me freaky thoughts.

He once tested me to see if I will come all the way across town to give him head while he got his car detailed. I showed up and showed out. All of his crew love me 'cause not only am I fly, I'm like big sis and I'm funny. It surprises them to see me always dressed up and I'm so down to earth. These factors, big girl and all, is what is winning New Jack over. I cook for him and make him feel special but he respects me because I am a go getta.

I bring to the table too. By him being so flashy, of course he wants to go to all the spots that are known in Dallas with me on his arm.

This led so many to believe that he is the head of his crew but it's the furthest from the truth. He kind of is one that got put on cause he been around these niggas for so long. The other three have that hustlers drive. He's the birdman of the group and RayRay is Slim, the real one with the paper. Yea he has the best shit but he don't know how to manage.

Overtime I will teach him valuable lessons on how to manage life and money. He loves that I'm kinky as hell, like for his birthday I got him a girl for me to watch him have sex with. While he fucks her brains out I sucked on his nuts and tossed his salad and sucked his toes while she rode him. Most of all he likes me because I allow New Jack to be him.

I can be just as flashy as him but when we are together we have fun. If he only knew that all of that fun is going to crush him. He dropped a few stacks on my new townhouse. He thought that I was staying with a girlfriend and needed my own place, but actually I have a house not far from his in DeSoto. It's gated so chances of him seeing me are slim.

Before I come home, I text him to see where he is. The only two cars he knows me to have is the Porsche Panermera and the Infiniti truck. He knows nothing about my 750 BMW. His house is very over the top and he has all the makings of young new black money .I'm cool with the realtor Kim Birdsong that sold it to him. For a quarter of a million, it was worth it, but he spent a lot upgrading itches can use a woman's touch, and in due time, the townhouse is what I will use as my storage shop for all my clients to come through. It's nice with three bedrooms and 2 1/2 baths. I have given him oral in damn near every room except the hot water closet. A couple of times, he has met his crew over there, and they discussed business.

At first, this was not liked by J-Money, but I come to learn that he is just a paranoid nigga and him and his crew should be 'cause we plan to bring them all down to their knees. I put on John Legend as I prepare for us to watch movies on Netflix and eat seafood. Jazz said she would try to come through with Ray Ray but who knows. Before New Jack gets here I need to call and touch bases with Naomi. She said things were getting hectic with Jamaica. Scoop said he got it under control when I text him earlier but I still want to check in with my gangsta bitch. Just as I finished with my call to her the doorbell rings followed by a text announcing New arrival.

Chapter 3: (Nyomi)

With a blunt on her freshly glossed lips, a Glock sitting on a white Louis Vuitton skirt and stacks of money on the table Naomi King is every bit of the part of a don as she handles the call.

"First off, who you say gave you my number bitch?" she asked

"George from Village Oaks." the female said nervously "OK ,second ,bitch I feel you on some dumb shit trying my patience cause this George clown and everybody in Dallas know I don't sell cookies. Bitch I move weight plain and simple .20 racks or better."

"Well he told me to get at you..."

"Well bitch where is this George?"

"Bitch fuck all that I just wanted to match the voice with the face and put a bitch on notice. That nigga who DM's you jumping in be sleep next to me and I wanted you to have it on your mind when you see me..."

"Bitch you know that's not the smoke you want. You silly bitches chasing these lame niggas. I don't chase nothing but a bag.

Diva's Revenge

You'll never catch me on a fool's side when I can be counting his paper poolside. Let that sink in on your way to child support court. See you when I see you. You know how I'm coming".

Naomi slams down the phone and go back to counting money to her helper Bobo she says "I don't know why these lame hos call my phone with the drama I know they know I'm a major bitch I make and break niggas in Dallas. I bleed the block in Balmain, and cut dope deals in Givenchy. I get my cars detailed in Lanvin and Armani."

"They don't know Naomi, they don't know" Bobo said as she passed back the blunt.

"I really been on some chill shit cause me and my girls got some shit going on but its hos like that, that make me put on my donkey suit. Naomi King was 24 and was a splitting image of Foxy Brown the rapper. She had all the right measurements with a couple of gold slugs in her mouth. All the hood love her and she was well respected business wise. They thought that at a young age she went to stay with her dad but she never left the hood she just had a strict Mama that work the dope scene in the South. She schooled Naomi very well on everything there is to know and taught her how to read people even when they said nothing.

For her 18th birthday her Mama gave her a brand new Dodge Charger, 3 keys of work and $5000. she told Naomi if you can't make this work the game is not for you but Naomi was already ahead of her Mama. She had been dipping in the hood and made some key connects because of her mom.

Naomi and her girls had their own agenda and things were going smoothly until Tasha caught that bullshit case but now things are in motion and going beautifully. She currently involved with Jamaica out of the crew. He's the reason we all are after his crew because he was a coward. Our dealings are very tricky for the crew. Scoop tells me that he is the wild cause of what his lingering over his head. He sells work and I started copping from him in order to get close to him but we have a few tricks to turn the tables and make it so he cops from me and my real man Magic.

Jamaica is very good looking and it's hard to stay on point around him. He looks like Allen Payne did back in his youth but what is even more the shit is his sex is off the chain. He loves to do anal sex and has no hang ups about oral sex. He is real passionate and has a lot of stamina.

We connect in a lot of other ways cause we both bleed the blocks. He sells me so much weight on wholesale and I make mine from serving the small timers. It works out for us both cause he is very limited with who he and his crew deal with. After the call I got earlier today in a matter of days that will all change between us. I've been fucking with him for a while now and his whole crew loves me to pieces I pretend not to know Jazz, Tasha or Mocha and we limit how much we come around each other.

Diva's Revenge

My man, my main man, is this nigga name Magic. The name alone describes him. I really get all of my dope from him but he gives me money to cop from Jamaica as part of the plan. Magic is like a legendary ghost in the hood everyone knows he exists because he fucks with all the major niggas but his way of business is very slick. No one actually sees him he wants to take over my hood but he don't have the muscle to take on Bozo or Jamaica, s crew. So he go use us to break both crews down. Bozo is no threat to me. But all that's going on now with Jamaica and his crew required a little more planning which is going on schedule from the phone call earlier.

I met Magic through my friend Romeo. One day I was in the mall shopping and I cut into Romeo. At first I blew him off because I didn't think the young nigga had it in him. Being a boss bitch from the hood I know how to read a nigga but Romeo flew under my radar and I totally misread the nigga. After talking to him I found his whole outlook similar to my own.

We started doing little deals here and there but one day he surprised me by asking if I was ready to make some real paper I told the nigga fuck yeah!!! He took me in what I thought was his only car a Chrysler 300 and took me to get his real car a white Maserati. From there we went and met with Magic. Magic then told me about him watching me and my crew operate and that he knew all about our agenda and feel he could be useful but nobody could have prepared me for what Magic and Romeo had in mind I arranged for Magic to meet the girls.

All of them was very pleased with his plan after that me and Magic became very close and he began to see the real Naomi that the streets never get. And through it all he loves me. He never makes demands that he wouldn't do. And even though he has way more money than I do he always makes me feel equal. I have keys to both of his houses plus the townhouse that we share.

Keys to all four cars and when I'm not getting us the latest shit from Tasha he takes me shopping all the time. He spoils me and puts me first. I often miss him when he goes to work but we talk all day .It was him that put the bow on our whole plan to bring down Jamaica and his crew and the added pluses both are good looking and have fire sex but where Jamaica is yella Magic is a shade from charcoal but he has perfect everything; teeth, nails his eyes on down to his dick.

He has the looks of DMX but the finesse of Denzel .Wears the best of the best that a lot of times even Tasha or Kricket can't get but he shows them love anyway on other shit. Romeo is his right hand. Boyish looks but man all the way. He's all about action he does little talking outside of to me or magic he pays attention to everything and hardly misses any details. He tells me all the time little Mama it's all about the details that make shit come together and it's that work ethic that I live by that has me and the crew as far along as we are.

3 days later...

"Yo Naomi I need you to come through now!" Jamaica yells through the phone.

"What's up Boo?" she replies innocently knowing full well what's up?

"Man shit is fucked up. Our connects spots just got hit this morning and right now Ray Ray is panicking real bad......"

"Slow down daddy. Don't you have a backup plan?"

"No my we've been dealing with him since we cut off Bozo and after the way we ended things with him we can't go back that way."

All this Naomi already knew but she had to be careful how she handled this conversation.

"So Jamaica what do you want me to do? I can come over. Let me wrap this up and I'm on my way"

"Man fuck all that shit get yo ass over here now because shit is hectic and I need to figure out what the fuck is up I'm at the spot with Ray Ray and J-Money .Text me when you close and be ready to fuck and suck some dick while I smoke a blunt and think.

Naomi smiled as she put her phone back down and looked at Magic and her girls

"So it begins. "She tells them.

Diva's Revenge

"I know I got the text with pics earlier." Jazz replied continuing "....we owe Uncle Mitch big for this."

"Yeah he might get some head for this."

"OK so now Naomi you go over and pitch dealing with me but you have to make it clear no face to face at all." Magic states.

"You already got his trust but to seal it make it look like you use your own money and he hit you back for it. Then see where it goes. I'm even going to go lower than this SA so when you offer it they can't refuse."

"Good idea I will get in J-money's ear I know he is gonna be the hardest." says Mocha.

"I'll do the same on Ray Ray ."Echoes Tasha.

"OK so everyone have their missions. Now let me go spark the flame. "Naomi breathe out as she get up and grab her Christian Dior bag.one by one the girls grab designer Fendi, Dolce Cabana and Prada bags in matching shades and all of them head out the door but before Naomi can go out the door Magic grabs her and kisses her, "Baby I love you .Are you sure you got it under control? If you want we can gorilla the niggas now. It's on you." Magic looks in her eyes.

"We come too damn far to turn back now daddy. It's balls to the wall. I want them to be brought to their knees. It's karma on my end. They both look at each other and smile as they recite its meaning; Keep Humiliating All Rich Motherfuckers Always.

Diva's Revenge

30 minutes later inside Jamaica's car...

Damn bitch you sucking that meat like this your last time or something. We lost our connect, not life in prison. Keep it up you gonna make that bitch throw up." Jamaica sees Ray Ray step outside just as he explodes in Naomi's mouth. He then asked her as he fixes his clothes "So this plug you got, he the truth or what?"

"Yeah I used to deal with him back in the day but I started fucking with you cause you had more weight. Well in that time the nigga done stepped his shit up and he been begging to fuck with me."

"I'm game but you got to sell that shit to them niggas in there."

"I got this daddy! Just shut up and let a bitch show you what's up and be ready for round two."

"I stay ready you go get lockjaw fucking with me." Jamaica said while pulling up his Rock and Republic jeans. As soon as they entered the house New Jack started with jokes.

"Don't come in here with dick breath trying to be in a nigga face."

"Shut the fuck up before I lick your face with it."

"Bitch it's too early for a headache."

"Who got a headache? I feel fine."

"You gonna have one you lick my face with that nigga dick on your breath."

34

"Anyways what's popping off? Man shit is hectic my plug got hit this morning".

RayRay sighs and interrupts.

"Jamaica told me." she replied and continued,

"OK look it's like this. I got a connect that I know from back when. He good people but doesn't want the spotlight. On good faith he gonna give me ten to show y'all he ready to do business. How much we will talk about that later. He is giving them to me at a steal cause we go back plus the more you buy the cheaper."

"I'm down!!" Jamaica exclaims.

"Of course yo tender dick ass gonna be down. "New Jacks states.

"What you think Ray Ray? J- Money?"

"I think if Naomi is so sure about him her and Jamaica should put the money up for the first ten then we go from there." Ray Ray says.

Then all of them turn to look at her and Jamaica .Without missing a beat Naomi agrees and Jamaica gives her a look like she was out of her mind. After a few seconds of silence finally J money spoke. "I don't know about this shit. I'm not trying to deal with all these extra ass motherfuckers. That's the shit getting niggas with a prison sentence." he says folding his arms.

"Nigga do you have any idea how to keep getting this money. You always think the worst."

"What you talking bout I'm trying to get money bitch. You better pump your brakes for a nigga do you in this bitch .I give zero fucks what you trying to do. I worry about my freedom. I didn't say I wasn't down. I'm just not as eager as your friendly ass is. Last time you stud up on me New Jack and I'm gonna put you on your pussy for real."

"You know what both of y'all shut the fuck up. Ain't nobody gonna do shit but do what we've been doing, get at this money and live the good life. Now if you need us on some beef shit y'all can catch the door."

As Naomi looks around the room. She locks eyes with J-Money she knows from that day forth he is the one to watch. They all smoke a blunt in silence then they all part ways .Naomi sends all of them the texts they been all waiting on. HIT DICE!!!! She drops her phone in her purse as they glide down 45 jamming Jeezy's new CD. She reaches over and pulls Jamaica dick out and leans over and begins to suck his dick to the sounds and as she goes for round two she smiled to herself at the thought of how easy these niggas are falling week.

Diva's Revenge

Whispers...
10 years ago...

"Mitch you mean to tell me that it's nothing in your reach that you can do look at the evidence dammit!" Mama Vi begins to Mitch. "Mama Vi I am only a street cop and I'm just now at five years. I can only say so much but I promise you I will make sure you know all developments."

"What the fuck is that? My son was beaten and then shot at point blank range by Jamaica and his nothing ass flunkies for friends. He has several bruises all over his body and it's no way one person could have did all that. On top of that....."

"Mama Vi, I'm on your side. Been on your side since I got the news, but what more can I do? No one in the hood is willing to step forward and go against these sons of bitches. So we are stuck at square one."

"No we not fucking stuck, y'all need to haul their asses in and beat the shit out of them. "

"What good would that do then, we would have a lawsuit to fight and Brian's case will be lost in the process? Just be patient Mama Vi. The truth and justice always seems to come when you least expect it."

"Patience?? How the fuck are you or anyone going to tell me to have patience? Was it you that had to bury your only child? No!!Was it you that has to sit day in and fucking day out and watch these streets act as this shit never happened? Is it you that get all the pity stares and head shakes when you go somewhere? No! It's not Mitch. Do you know how hard it is to live in this house with all of my memories? Every time I see them four pieces of shit I am enraged. As they ride around with Bozo in their fancy cars and clothes, smoking their blunts, my heart breaks. When I realized that my baby is never coming home again..."

"Mama Vi you can't beat yourself up over this. You did everything a good mother supposed to do and more. We all knew you loved Brian and you knowing that should allow you to sleep at night."

Mitch gave Mama Vi long hug and wiped away her few remaining tears. They promised to keep in touch and Mitch walked back to his car. As he did he looked around at the neighborhood that for so long he had been proud to be from. How could they treat Tanesha as they have? Yeah I know that Tanesha was not day one from here but after eight years everyone had embraced her as theirs. Okay, so she crossed the line in deceiving Jamaica but was a bullet to the head right? I can even understand jumping on her cause when I grew up as a homosexual there was a rite of passage but no one is God and decides who dies. It's only so much I can tell Mama Vi that will keep me from incriminating myself but I know justice will be served if it's the last thing I do. All four of those boys will each learn the power of an angry black gay man.

Meanwhile......

"Girl that is so sad how they found Tanesha. It scared me so bad I don't even want to go to the store no more and that was one of my favorite spot cause they still sell the bacon with the rind on it." chatted the women.

"Girl you talking about Rhoton's on Lancaster? Bitch I didn't know that's where they found her." said Denise.

"Yeah and everybody knows Jamaica and his crew did it too." added Fancy.

"How the fuck you crackhead bitches know so much?" the woman asked.

"Bitch cause when I ain't puffing I be listening to the streets. Info cost money and it keeps me high too. Ain't that right!" Denise says in between high fives to Fancy.

"Yep speaking of let's go." Said Fancy.

The woman eyed both of them until they were out of sight. She always talks to them on her porch. Yeah she grew up with them but a crack head is a crackhead and they can't be trusted. She picked up the phone and called her daughter to see how she was doing at her dad's house for the weekend.

"Hey baby. How's mama's baby doing over there? Yo daddy ain't got any of them nasty bitches around does he?"

Diva's Revenge

"No Mama we having fun with Uncle Fred and his kids." replied Rah-Rah

"Did you tell your daddy about what Jamaica and his crew done. Tell him even the crackheads know they done it."

"Mama Daddy said he knows all of that and for you to mind your own business."

"Well I was thinking he could use that to finally take down Bozo. He the one saying Bozo is making it hard to get to a bag and I'm just making sure that my baby stays in the best shit."

"Yeah right Mama and then he pays your rent and car note on the first. He told me all that. I got to go I'll see you Sunday."

"Make sure you tell your daddy tired ass to give you money for school for the week."

"I know Mama and you know you love my daddy still." After the call was over she sat there and thought of the man she gave up so much for. It was this hatred towards him that made her do everything in her power to teach Rah-Rah what it takes to be a boss bitch. I want Rah-Rah to grow up to know how to get and keep a boss nigga. I wasn't able to keep the one I had cause of my mouth but I'll be damned if Rah-Rah miss hers.

<u>Diva's Revenge</u>

Meanwhile....

As I closed the phone on my momma crazy ass I smile at her motivation. She only wants the best for me and from watching all her mistakes in dealing with my dad I know what I got to do to keep a baller. When I grow up my mission is to be the Queen of Dallas dope girls and I have a few tricks up my sleeve to guarantee all this. All I have to do is start to be around the majors in order to get my feet wet. OH how I love the hood!!!.

Diva's Revenge

Chapter 4... New Jack

As a young nigga in the hood you learn all the rules of the game from the older cats then it's up to you if yo ass applied it. I was blessed that my potna Corey big brother was a known nigga in the hood. He took a liking to me and my boys J-Money and Angel and he showed us the ropes when it started and it was us four young niggas but Corey couldn't take the heat and he went the completely other direction and stayed in school .Ray Ray was his brother an when we came through he always showed us love. He noticed me out of everyone because I was the loudest and my mom was one of few women in the hood that held a good job and by me being her only child I was spoiled.

Ray Ray was older than all of us by five years and ran with a major nigga in the hood named Bozo. In my eyes Ray Ray was the man because he had more than me but later in the game I came to see things very differently. He gave Corey anything he wanted and this made Corey very popular in the hood but I was the nigga in the group with the looks. Corey and Ray Ray both are ugly niggas but they had a ton of swag.

Because my mom had a full time job my house was the party house. No one in the hood liked my mom cause they thought she was uppity. It wasn't that she just was always busy. By her being the outcast no one told her what I was up to while she was gone. My house was the spot in the hood majority of the niggas i smashed their first piece of pussy. It was also the place where a lot of beef started and my front yard was where a lot of shit went down in the hood.

I never really got involved except this one time that this new nigga in the hood had to be taught a lesson. Ray Ray told me and my boys about this nigga trying to move in in the hood and take shit over. RayRay explained to us that by doing this nigga he could set us up in the hood for life.

To this day no one can really remember his name cause only thing everyone kept talking about was his candy Apple red Toyota Camry. Anyway the nigga had words with Ray Ray and pulled a gun on Ray Ray. At the time Ray Ray was on papers and couldn't afford the heat plus Bozo said doing him personally would drop too much heat, so me and my boy set the nigga up and beat his ass.

We broke his nose, knocked out his teeth and broke his arm. Then in front of everyone in the middle of the hood we

44

burned his car. We at the time didn't know that he had just used all his money to re up and it was all in the car. All we knew was a lesson needed to be taught and that scared the shit out of Corey. He totally slid back from us and when he did hang around it wasn't on the same level now as before. Depending on who tells the story, most people say I'm the leader of our group, but there is no leader.

Out of us three I'm the one that loves to party and have a good time. I love clothes and cars and all the pussy a nigga can stand. The love of clothes and pussy is how I made this bitch Tasha my main bitch. I normally don't go for big girls but I never see the difference cause she handles shit as good as these skinny bitches and the ho is a true go getter and niggas value that type of bitch. With her I feel that she the one but I have to take things slow in order to tame her a bit.

She hang with this stuck up ho name Jazz. Her face looks familiar but I have yet to place it. I cook for these hos cause they are down for us. Jamaica and J-Money done bag them some nice hos too. It's good to finally cut into some hos that Bozo and his crew haven't ran through. It's funny how Ray Ray and Bozo used to once be tight but now they arch enemies. Bozo used to serve Ray Ray. And in turn that's how he met J-Money and Jamaica but when Ray Ray got busted and went to jail that was probably the best look a nigga could have had cause he caught back up with his homie from boot camp. He promised Ray Ray that he would put him on and we been on ever since.

The beef started because instead of Bozo being player about the come up, he got out in his chest over it. At first Bozo was cool but once he seen how much more we were getting and how smooth we ran our ship the nigga flipped. He started showing up at Spud's and flexing. He would come to different events in the hood and make problems, but his pride would never let him say why he was so upset. I mean of course niggas knew, but we wanted to hear him say it to our faces. His crew of niggas fuck with three bad ho's that are on they shit but I feel our ho's are about to smash their reputation in the hood.

Cheatah been with Bozo for a while and they are good together. She is a bad bitch by most standards but she fucked up and let Bozo know he got her. She hangs with Rah-Rah. Shanky and Scooter been together since junior high. And Rah-Rah been with Melly Mel just as long. All three ho's be on their best shit and it's not really no ho's in the hood that's been able to touch them. Melly Mel and Scooter are two of the dumbest niggas I know. Why because they still depend on Bozo to make shit happen for them.

When those niggas could have been gone on, they both keep it player when they see me mobbing in the hood and really it's just Bozo that has the issue. The nigga has a lot of shit but we have almost more cause it's four of us. At first I thought things were doomed after my connect got popped but Naomi saved the day for us. I like the bitch cause she thorough and she understands the streets. She get what a nigga is trying to do plus the Ho get out there and get in a Ho shit. On more than one occasion I watched her beat the shit out of a bitch.

I even seen her dome a nigga. She is well respected in the hood to be honest with you. The squad we have built is pretty certified. We do our best shit. Only person I worry about is Jamaica. The nigga seems to have a hidden agenda.

I mean we all have shit that we fucked up about, but the hood got us. I mean we was kind of fucked up with him about the shit with Tanesha, but when he explained and told us what he wanted to do, we handled it without any hesitation. I don't know maybe this Ho Naomi will get his ass back on track. If anybody can do it it's her. Now as far as my bitch, she solid. Jazz is really our secret weapon. She smart and got the looks. Most smart bitches never look good but my bitch got it all. Mocha looks like an exotic Barbie but she cool. Now if we could just get them all on point and on the same page.

Jamaica.....

Coming up in this hood I feel like I was always having to prove some shit by me having good looks. A nigga being mixed caused all kinds of problems. My mom started fucking around with J-Money mom and we became real tight. Corey was my boy too cause we always were in the same classes growing up. Everybody was cool with New Jack as his house was the party house. A lot of niggas ran through that house but Corey ran with us, cause he wanted to be like his brother. What I liked about Corey is he was quiet and really don't make much noise. The nigga sits back in the cut and laughs but he is far from dumb.

New Jack is the clown in the group. He's the one that breaks the ice with Ho's and most of the time he will be the one that starts the conversation up. He's the flashy one and I tell him all the time to calm down. It does not help much that he bagged this booster bitch Tasha, cause now she got his head blown up. I mean I give the bitch props, she got our whole squad on point.

None of these cats can fuck with us. Really it's a couple of niggas from the Nawf that is on their best shit but otherwise no. J-Money be on some paranoid shit that really I should be on. I mean after this whole Tanesha shit I just knew I was doomed but Ray Ray knew what to do. He is the levelheaded one out of us all and the only thing is I don't want this beef with Bozo to blow up into what we got going.

Shit will really blow up if they knew J-Money was smashing Cheetah. J-Money thinks no one knows but I know cause I seen him at the same fuck off spot I used to go to with Tanesha before the drama. All this shit is too much at times for me and I don't want any parts. I really am trying to get my money up and burn off before this Tanesha shit blows up but I guess these niggas forgot my objective.

I mean my bitch Naomi is a good distraction cause she is everything a nigga been needing but I can't do no time for this shit. I'm too young to go down I have my whole life ahead of me. Give me three or four more months and I'll be ready but I'll be damn it seems like every time I'm close to where I want to be to burning off, something always pops up and pushes me back.

Maybe I'm just being paranoid, cause it's been all this time, 10 years and nothing has happened in the Tanesha thing. I got too much shit that I have gained. I have my health and a nice four bedroom house, I have three cars and money what else could a nigga want? But I get tired of looking over my shoulder. I know that my niggas fuck with me but at times I feel like they think less of me. That's why it was crucial that I bag Naomi, to shut these niggas up, but what made it an added bonus was this bitch is really plugged in.

At crunch time this bitch stepped all the way up because we were all lost after Ray Ray's connect got popped. J-Money still got his issues but he can't deny the shit been on point and we doing good. J-Money comes across a lot of times like he got shit on his chest that he wants to get off. These niggas think cause I'm yella and mixed that I won't get on they shit, but out of everybody, J-Money knows better.

Him and New Jack was there when I beat this one nigga's ass. I just be chilling and now since we all got Ho's that's about something, we about to take over the hood and certain niggas know it. It just seems like all these things fell into place too perfectly and at times I wonder is this all a dream.

J-Money....

I love my niggas like they my real brothers but even brothers get tired of each other. Right now my crew is at the top of everything but when I look at how shit going, I know trouble is about to happen. Then when I say this nigga calls me paranoid, but I pays attention. Each of my niggas have their weaknesses and I will tell you about them. Mine is I miss out on so much life because I can't stop and enjoy shit.

I just can't relax knowing it's a grimy ass nigga waiting around the corner to get what I got. I'm an average looking nigga but I'm always well groomed. I take real good care of my body and I smoke weed but that's it.

I try not to cause any extra attention to me. I have a nice truck and car but I kept them factory like the niggas up North do. No flashy rims or paint jobs. My house is in a modest part of Cedar Hill. But on the inside I went all out. I dress really nice but I wear shoes like Berluti and Cole Haan.

I don't rock shit that has the logo stamped across the clothes. Niggas look like clowns with all these stunts stamps all over them. Money recognize money. My boy New Jack's girl says she likes my taste. She keeps all of us on our best shit. I like that we all are now chilling with one Ho. All these different random chicks becomes hard to tell who out to get you. I know I'm content with my Ho, Mocha. She is the right amount of freak that I like. She is a stripper, but I plan on changing that for good. She keep this dick like she do and licking on me like I like and she can stay in her place, she gonna be good.

New Jack is the one I worry about. He too damn flashy. And his mouth is too much at times, but that's my nigga though. I pay attention to his moves and he pisses me off a lot. A lot of people in the hood thinks he runs our crew but he's the furthest thing from it. If anything its Ray Ray and Jamaica. Ray Ray's the one that put us all on. And Jamaica and his Ho, Naomi, saved us real shit. My nigga Jamaica is real fosho, but first when the bullshit popped off about Tanesha I thought the nigga was funny style but then he put in his work and never looked back.

I mean I understood cause the bitch even fooled me and I know how to spot them niggas anywhere. Ray Ray is the truth and I can never repay him for all the love he has shown us. He taught me so much about life. It was him that brought my first piece of pussy to New Jack's Mama's house. He even coached me before on what to do. I remember jumping when he made the Ho give all of us some head in the living room. But now I'm the truth. My sex game is a fool. It's just after Ramona poked holes in the condoms to try to trap me I don't trust none of these Hos.

I feel they are out to get me but I stay one step ahead and only get ahead. Mocha make me want more but in time we shall see. I give Ray Ray his props, that nigga a major nigga, but he always had ugly Ho's until this Ho Jazz. I told him he would be dumb as fuck not to keep her. She's smart, fly, and pretty. The Ho has her shit together and you can tell she with him because she likes him. All of our Ho's are a perfect fit and we got things on lock. Now if I can just shake this Ho, Cheatah. She got some good pussy, but our beef with Bozo is getting bad and if this nigga find out, let alone if my crew find out and I didn't tell them....but the pussy and power is so good.

RayRay

I have an advantage over a lot of niggas in the hood. I have the gift of hindsight. I am able to look at things from more than one angle. This is key in the hood because without it, you are not likely to survive and I've been surviving by being able to outthink these lame cats. As a young nigga that was bigger than the rest I got snatched up by Bozo, a neighborhood legend. He gave me knowledge on a lot of things in life but his downfall was he didn't want me to grow. He wanted me as a man to be codependent on him and that's not cool at all.

Diva's Revenge

Now when I first started out, I was his gopher and muscle. I would light a nigga ass up at the drop of the dime and after a while it grew into pistol play. I was fearless and Bozo liked that. Scooter and Melly Mel was cool cats, they just had no backbone and I knew they would forever be under Bozo. But not me, my mission was to soak up all that I could from him about the game and stack my paper and burn rubber. But Bozo wasn't tryna hear that, he only exposed me to so much. He never let me meet his connects. He never gave me enough work that I would hurt him if I burned him. In other words, he spoon fed me along. It was all good because I fucked a lot of Ho's and made a name for myself in the process.

I had to build up my own crew of niggas because I knew that the day would come where I no longer needed Bozo. I have a younger brother named Corey and although I would love for him to be under me I want him to go to school even more. But his three boys are most definitely what I need.

They all got that young nigga itch and hunger that is needed on the street. When I first started looking at them, New Jack kind of rubs me wrong and to this day he don't know how close he came to losing all his teeth in his front yard. He had a bad habit when bitches around trying to roast other niggas. He did this to me and my brother but after J- Money stopped him and when he looked at me he got the hint. "Nigga you better pump yo brakes before I pump four or five in you. I know I'm an ugly nigga but I got a big dick and deep pockets and I know how to treat a bitch".

It's just about trusting one to get close to me. Now that I got Jazz, I think that is over with. She is certified but that's a story for later on. Now because those niggas were going to have my life in their hands, I had to test their hearts. So once I got the niggas to get in the game I had to see if they was about that life or just riding my dick for hood fame.

It was this nigga that started coming around and he really was no threat and really wanted to get on but he just rubbed me wrong. We called the nigga Camry cause that's what he drove. The nigga shit was on point. I decided to test my crew to see how they were operating. I lied to the niggas and told them that Camry owed me some money and that when I confronted him he drew down on me. The little young niggas was more than ready to do this nigga on the block in front of the hood.

I was especially shocked by Jamaica. When they got to the block they had Corey with them. They approached Camry and of course the nigga Camry got fly and they remembered I said he had a gun, so the niggas took off on him beating the shit out of him, knocking out his teeth and setting his car on fire. The car was overkill. If we only knew that the nigga stash was in there. The Nigga left town and the crew got they props. This also scared the shit out of my brother. To show them some love me and Bozo took the niggas to the mall and got them a couple polo outfits and the newest Jordans.

I still remember New Jack capping to Ho's about it. "Yeah a nigga know I'll beat that ass. I'm a fool with these hands." Ray Ray laughed at the thought cause he did the least, out of fear of getting his clothes dirty. All of my boys serve a purpose. They are all loyal to me. It would crush them to know that I purposely started a beef with Bozo to start a war to take the hood and get us street credit. In the hood it can only be one up top and that can't be shared. The nigga Bozo would never share the throne with me and I could not dream of sharing my connect with him. So when I was sure that I was in good with my Mexican homie I started some drama with Bozo. It started with a very simple text message

"Where you at".

This is how Bozo knew I had his money. His reply will be "who is this"?

I will soon let him know it was me. He already knew it was me but it was part of our code. Normally after I stated who I was he would then ask me "where was I"?

This is very crucial for us because we had meeting spots on all freeways. But each freeway told how much work I was wanting. Normally I will either say 45 freeway for five keys of dope or 635 meant 10. But today the text went different. "I'm at home chilling"

His reply was "call me ASAP" so I did.

"What's good?"

"Shit you tell me, before I can even find out you on lock, yo ass out and on the move. I guess you finally put yo dick in the right Ho." Bozo joked. "

"Something like that. So all I owe you is 16 for the last and the charge from the Houston deal right?" Ray Ray asked.

"Yeah that put us at 19. What's up Ray Ray shit don't feel right?" Bozo questioned.

"Well you know it just comes a time when a nigga gotta jump off the porch."

"So what you saying you not fucking with me no more. Nigga you know I made you. What you go do without me"? Bozo says with the tone of ridicule.

"See that's what's wrong with you bitch niggas. You may got Scooter and Melly Mel on lock. But not this nigga. I am a man and I am also a beast. Now I tried to be cool about it 'cause I know you ain't got it in you to do no gangsta shit but now. I'm gonna tell you like this, get in my way and I'll run through you like diarrhea. In this game it's no room to share the top." Ray Ray exclaimed.

"So nigga are you saying that we on some other shit? Nigga I would have let...."

"Bitch let? How the fuck you feel you gonna let a stump down nigga like me do a motherfucking thing Nigga? I'm the reason you even walking in the hood still. Niggas been wanting to rob you but didn't want to see me!" Ray Ray retorted.

Bozo laughs, "That's funny 'cause I gave a nigga a "Key" not to smoke you and New Jack at a dice game."

"Look yo time done expired and you wasting money and time spit boxing. Just stay out my way and I'll allow you continue to eat." Ray Ray threatened then added "Oh and tell Cheetah to stay out the Red Door motel 'cause I seen her." Ray Ray says this as he clicks off his phone.

As he sits back and thinks about it, he knows that wasn't the way to go out with Bozo but he also knew that Bozo is a very jealous nigga and once he seen what he was bringing in, the beef would eventually start. I know that me and my crew is on our best shit. I laugh as I think how most people think it's New Jack that runs our crew. I like it like that.

It's a strategy I picked up from the Japanese. When the boss has a meeting or goes out in public he never lets people come straight to him. He sends someone else to do his talking and he sits back and observes all movements. This frame of mind and approach is what has kept me ahead of the game. It's really him and Jamaica that run shit. Naomi was a lifesaver with her connect.

Really all the girls that my crew done started fucking with is the truth. Each girl brings something to the table and holds me and my niggas down. I know Tasha and Jazz are tight but I hope they get along with Mocha and Naomi. Naomi so hood that bitch is crazy, but ever since I started seeing her in the hood I knew she was gangster now I'm seeing more closely and I like what I'm seeing. Mocha is a stripper and really she doing her best shit 'cause J-Money been on some chill shit. He said the Ho keeps him drain and that is always a good thing. All in all my crew is doing our best shit and about to put the hood on lock.

Chapter 5: Jazmine Omega

If I had to describe me in one word it would be devastating. Why? Because all that I possess is not easily seen by the naked eye. I, at 24, am a graduate from Texas Southern University with a PHD in medicine. Of course guys are drawn to me because of my looks, I am a deep Brown skin and all of my measurements fit with my 5-6 frame. It's easy for me to find clothes for my size 2 frame and shoes for my size 7 feet. I have great hair and skin that I am a fanatic about keeping on point but most guys are devastated because I have street smarts.

My family is from the same hood that my girls are from. It's just my mother convinced my father at an early age to move us out but I stayed in the hood schools cause my family all went there. I was able to stay connected without living in it. We moved to Cedar Hill when I was 14 and really to this day it all seemed to happen all of a sudden for us.

Diva's Revenge

One day I was chilling in the hood and the next I'm not. My mother says after Tanesha was killed the hood changed for the worse. I think she was scared I would get caught up. She would have a stroke if she knew who I was dating now. But I have to. I made a vow with my girls and my life has been dedicated to this mission. I even chose my career for this mission. I work at Tri-City Memorial Hospital way outside the hood to fly under the radar because Jasmire Omega in the hood is not what you get at work and I want to keep the two separate.

I normally go for really clean cut guys that look like Pharrell Williams and Ray Ray is so far from that. He is so ugly till it's unreal, but he was blessed with swag and that love of swag is going to be his and his crew's demise. From what Scoop told me about Ray Ray, he only got with "good girls". No hoodrats for him. If he even suspect you one, it's out of there for you. He wants bitches that are square because he doesn't want to stress over two people's hustles, just his. He is the head of his crew and makes things happen for them and his reputation is what keep niggas off their ass.

Before they got where they are, he was known to be muscle for Bozo. While doing time he cut into the right Mexican and him and his crew been on ever since. Because of this, he loves the best of everything from cars to food, to clothes, and everything in between. During my upbringing I was blessed to be around nice things, so it's in me to look nice. I go to Ah-Donis weekly to get my hair done and I get all the upscale clothes from my girl Tasha and her partner Krickett. They keep us in BCBG runway stuff, Fendi, Chanel, St. John and other favorites like Balmain and Alexander Wang.

Tasha and Krickett are two of the baddest big girls I seen. They always look Hollywood ready and because they love clothes so much they are good at what they do. Krickett is known for always rocking the latest Diane Von Furstenberg dresses and the latest IT bags.

Me, I'm more simple like Kourtney Kardashian. You have to know your shit to know what I am in. My goal is to always look rich. All of this came into play because with Ray Ray he is anything but conventional. He and his crew don't really do clubs. He knows to plan a meeting around it so I had to make a chance meeting happen.

I was with Tasha when she was going to meet him and New Jack to buy some clothes. I was like a supermodel on her off day as I sat in the passenger seat of Tasha's Porsche Panarema. I played with my IPhone and acted as if none of them mattered. I was in a simple Chloe dress, maxi of course, with some Jimmy Choo gladiator sandals and big Jackie O wraparound Chanel shades. Behind those shades I am watching his every move as him and New Jack pour through what Tasha brings. She got the latest Ralph Lauren and Hugo Boss as well as a few Robert Graham shirts like Jay-Z wears. They are very pleased to say the least and that's why Tasha and her crew are the best in Texas. I patiently waited for my intro and I got it when New Jack and Tasha started play flirting and kissing.

"Excuse me Miss Lady are we taking up too much of your time?" Ray Ray asks

This moment is crucial because my reply can either kill it or bring it to life. From Scoop I know he likes a bit of a challenge so I can't come off as too eager to talk.

"No I'm just checking on some patient stats for work." she replied.

"What kind of patients?" said Ray Ray

"I'm a doctor, sweets. Anymore questions from.... what was your name while you all up in my business. "Jazz snap back.

"You hot about some shit, you PMSing or something and my name is Ray Ray. Tasha never told me about you I guess she wanted you to be a secret."

"Well I didn't know she had to list all friends in order to sell a thug some clothes and my name is Jasmine Omega. Doctor Jasmine Omega and when I figure out if you gonna rob me or not I may let you start to call me Jazz like everyone." With eye roll Jazz extended her hand to him.

"I don't know if medicine was your calling Lil' Mama cause you would be perfect doing comedy. Is there any way I can convince you that I am not gonna rob you of anything but maybe your heart?"

"Slow down, go fast. How do you know I don't have a man or that you my type? "She asked as she cocked to the side to lean on the door in Tasha's car.

"You right, but you can't be happy cause you gave me too much airtime for a lady that's content."

"What else can I do, you being a local thug I'm sure you got like 3 or 4 crazy "baby mothers" lurking around?" Ray Ray burst out laughing and couldn't control himself.

Finally jazz ask what's so funny despite knowing.

"Doctor O it's not called "mothers" in the hood, its "Baby Mamas" and I have one child that I take very good care of, like anything or anyone that I choose to be in my life. Secondly, no I'm not involved with these Ho's around here with all their hidden agendas.

Now it was Jazz's turn to laugh because she knew that he really was talking about her and her crew. As they talk, she avoids all of his advances and makes him feel like less than a man in an undermining way. He asked real pointed questions that the real Jazz loved to hear from a man, but as part of the script she fed him what he needed to hear.

She couldn't help but notice that when she would check her phone he would take the time to appraise her from head to toe and that was cool, which is why Tasha took an extra-long time with New Jack today.

Diva's Revenge

"When I felt I had him where I wanted him I will text Tasha that I'm ready and she will come and we would purposely leave without any way for him to reach me but through Tasha".

He asked me a very weird question that the average bitch would have fumbled the ball but Scoop had already prepared me for his way of thinking.

"How do you feel about men like me? Would you give up your career to support me?"

Without hesitation Jazz replied, "Love is not a thing that can be easily navigated. Dating, I'm more selective about the men I keep company with. Honestly I feel like a thug couldn't win me over because of his limited scope on life." she said while looking up dead in his eyes. This statement not only pissed him off but after that day it made getting her as his, his sole mission. Once I saw that I had made my point I texted Tasha.

She came out giggling with New Jack. He quickly said, "Jazz I'm surprised you still here having to look at this ugly ass nigga. They all laugh. New Jack was looking nice in his linen pants and casual polo Versace shirt with Bally sandals. Ray Ray wasn't too bad neither, he was covered head to toe in Gucci nonetheless. He smelled good and was wearing the latest Jean Paul cologne.

As Tasha started the car we all exchanged goodbyes. Tasha and New Jack's were a little more intimate. As we got on I-20, Tasha got the text we both knew was coming. Ray Ray asking her if she would hook us up. Tasha quickly told him she didn't know if I would be game and when she got time she would get at him. Not even an hour later Tasha got a text from New Jack that sealed the deal......

This nigga is out of there. He can't stop talking about DR. O and he ain't even smelled the pussy. Please do yo thang ma, for this nigga kill us both OMG SMH.

Tasha smiled when I passed her back her Galaxy, we sat and talked while we smoked a blunt on our way to eat at The Cheesecake Factory. Over the next few weeks when Tasha went to sell him and his crew things, he went out of his way to be in pocket when Tasha came through. He even gave her an extra thousand dollars to wait an hour while he handled some business. When he finally made it he drilled Tasha about me and my likes.

Normally he is very set on what he likes but now he asks Tasha would I like it. It was nothing that he had dismissed the hoodrats, but rumor had it that he really wanted to be with Cheetah, the same bitch that is me and my crew rivals. But lately they are saying that when she comes around he pays her no mind. Scoop said he told everyone he planned to "wife" me. After being elusive for so long I set it up to call Tasha while she was around them after a month of torture. Tasha yells at the phone to me "Hold on Jazz let me get this shit out my hand."

Tasha cut her eyes to see RayRay freeze all his movements. She laughs but it's too late because before she knows it he is in her face.

"Tasha baby girl please let me say two words to her."

"Girl is you trying to talk to Ray Ray? He loves you." Giggles Tasha.

"Girl put him on." Jazz says.

"Two words Keith Sweat." Tasha mocks.

"Dr. O you are a very hard lady to get near and you got better protection that the president." Tasha hits him in the arm playfully and pretends to reach for her phone. But New Jack is already on top of things and grabs her by the waist and drags her off kissing and whispering on her neck. They laugh while Ray Ray gets his airtime. Instantly he starts in on how hard it is to get at me and how he can't get me out of his mind.

"So how can I get to know you a little better?" RayRay laments.

"What's your number and I'll text you and we can go from there?" Jazz already knew his working number so this was critical what he gave her as that would tell how serious he was. When Jazz heard the first three numbers a smile as big as it was when she graduated came across her face.

Jazz spent countless hours texting him over the next weeks. Her, Scoop and the girls spent just as much time going over them. Our first date was really me inviting him to "my house". I cooked for us and we watched TV. For a thug that do so much shit on the run that's what he wants with his girl, to slow it down. We watched all the ratched reality shows and he was at full attention.

They are my favorite shows but I played dumb and allowed him to bring me up to speed. We fell asleep in each other's arms watching The Chi. The place was nice and the furniture comfortable but it was far from my home in Valley Ranch near where the Dallas Cowboys use to practice. Scoop said this place is better because it's close to Downtown. In Valley Ranch I know too many people and that could cause a few problems. He often brings me clothes and bags that he cops from Tasha.

I laugh because it is shit I already have. I take it back to Tasha to exchange it for other things. Shit has really gotten serious because now he wants me to ride along with him to "check on shit". Which is how he describes what him and his crew does. At this point, I have to really be careful because even though I know Mocha and Naomi, I can only pretend to know Tasha. We should all be good because we keep each other on point about movements. He is starting to demand more of my time and has started leaving things with me as if he sure there is a tomorrow with us. I welcomed all of that. I even kept one of his T-Shirts to walk around in when he comes over.

Diva's Revenge

I thought he would jump out of his mind when he offered to pay for my hair and Ah-Donis told him it was $650. But he paid for it and he tipped her fifty dollars. It really was shocking me that he was doing all this. He even stays true when I'm not around. But all of this is what Scoop told us, which is why he requires the most attention. He is the brains to this whole operation and once she is in good graces, the others will follow. Tasha has New Jack in her web also. It's really Mocha that I'm most worried about. Yea, we all grew up together but she has a different outlook on things.

It's almost time for us to move on to the next phase. Scoop and the girls are very pleased with how I'm doing. Ray Ray is known in the hood to be very elusive and hard to get close to. Jamaica, J-Money and New Jack all have they weaknesses that any woman can penetrate but Ray Ray is cut from a different cloth. He often leaves me horny for him but we all agreed to play the "saving for marriage" card.

Sex with him would be too intense and complicate matters. Even oral sex with him would be over whelming. Who knows that may be one rule I break. Another unique thing about him is that he is really close to his son. So I have to be very careful because kids are hard critics at times and it could hurt things. What's fucking me up is how nice Ray Ray is turning out to be towards me. It's hard to believe at times that he's the monster I know him to be. But when I need to be snapped out of my daze, I look at my friend Tanesha picture, and hold it close to my heart.

As I go through my closet to get my outfit ready for our date, I am undecided on whether to fuck his head up with this Cavalli dress or go for class with this badass pantsuit from Dior. While I go through all of this stuff in my mind, I smoke a blunt and call Scoop. Scoop will know how to play it. He always knows what to do.

Diva's Revenge

Chapter 6: Champion Lounge

In every hood around the world they all got that one spot that everybody goes to show their status to the hood. It marks you for life cause at any given time, an incident can transpire that can shape your whole life. It can make or break your street cred too. In our hood everyone goes to Champion Lounge. It's the biggest club we got and it's where we all go to show off. It's got four VIP booths that all the baller niggas jockey to get first dibs at every weekend.

Once a year right before Thanksgiving the club has a big party for the hood. This is your time to show out and do your best shit. We put together things for the whole year in preparation of this event. Tasha and her crew have been really busy with all the demands of everyone and she feels it's going to be very interesting to see how everyone come through. This night at the club marks one year that the crew and the girls have all been together officially and this will be the first time all of them will be in the same room at one time. Money is coming in like a waterfall and they are all eating.

Diva's Revenge

Ray Ray and New Jack have a trick up their sleeves to upset the whole night. They just got a brand new Rolls Royce Ghost and Bentley Mulsane. No one will expect them to have these. They are used to the Ashton and other cars they have. Ah-Donis shop has been crazy with all the girls wanting some exotic shit for the party. All the girls scheduled their shit around the same time but with 20 minute gaps so not to bring any more suspicion.

Everything must be perfect cause this night is when the hood will know that Bozo is no longer supreme. Everybody is busy with different forms of preparation. The girls all met up for what they call their "spa day". It's when they meet up and pamper themselves along with going to scheduled doctor's appointments. It's during this routine stop for the girls that could mean the end as Denise and Fancy are in the alley behind the clinic and see the girls together.

Fancy was too busy getting high, but Denise put two and two together and rushed Fancy back to the hood to tell Bozo about their discovery.

"Man, Denise what you want with your everlasting crazy ass?" Bozo laughs

"That's OK, I may be crazy but this old bitch know her shit." Denise replies and continues, "you not gonna believe what I found out. But it's gonna cost you."

"Bitch I knew your lame ass was on some grimy shit." Bozo barked.

"Yeah but you will thank me." Denise grins.

"I'm listening."

"Naomi is fake, her and her crew. I got proof that she fake as hell." Denise declares.

"Look I know Naomi and been knowing the bitch. You better watch your mouth before one of these young Ho's hear you and tell her cause you know you don't want to see her. And what crew you talking about?" Bozo questions.

"Those girls she be with." replied Denise.

"See it might not been her cause that bitch mobs with that bitch nigga Jamaica."

"I know but them Ho's she with and her are all fake. They not real." Denise pleads.

"So what bitch. Let me guess yo smoker ass real. Get the fuck out of here. Here's two dollars, go do something with yourself, man you tripping for a dime hit" Bozo fires at her.

"I don't need your money, I was trying to put you on point but mark my words it's gonna come back to haunt you." she says.

"Girl we ain't got no money you better take that, we need it." Fancy says.

"We don't need him. Fuck hi...." before Denise knew what hit her one of Bozo goons knocked her out. She was yet another example of the hood and its code. Bozo got a real laugh out of this although it was all funny he would keep an eye out for shady shit.

Meanwhile across town each girl got their hair done at Ah-Donis shop. She pulled out all stops and each girl got styles that added to what they were going to be wearing that night. As they were admiring each other hair at the shop Jazz got a text from Saks personal shopper alerting her that all of their bags for the party were finally in. Plus, Tasha got all them Louboutin's on her trip to New York. But, Mocha in true prostitute form, was going to rock some $3000 over the knee Blumarine Python boots. To give her look an exotic feel she went with a Brazilian 3D lace in black and Brown that came down to her ass.

She found a really nice Dior white leather mini dress and a gold belt. She was carrying a huge Bottega bag that matched her boots. Now Jazz was a milder version with long windswept hair winged out like the Kardashians made famous with a side swept bang. Her Louboutin's were simple except the red bottom and she decided to wear a black Givenchy top with connected scarf. All sexy and understated with a simple metallic and black Balmain skirt. She also decided to rock a huge Ferragamo bag.

Tasha couldn't pass up the chance to show out for all big girls. She buzzed all her hair off and dyed it. It's spiked in a sexy pixie that compliments her face. She chose some huge Chanel earrings and a Balmain skirt set and underneath the hot pink suit she's wearing a vintage YSL Tee shirt. All of these things matches her

Louboutin's that are sky high peep toe in pink. Her bag is an alligator Birkin bag that was 4000 itself.

Naomi recently has become obsessed with all things Jeremy Scott of Moschino, so she washead to toe in it. She got the newest stuff that has the name in gold armor on black leather. She decided to change it up from her usual lengthy hair in go for a Nicki bob that has streaks on it and because she is always ready for a fight, she rocked a small crossbody bag and strap up the legs shoes. One thing is for sure, if hopping out of a Mulsane and Ghost ain't enough to upset them, what they wearing and the niggas on their arms will.

Ah-Donis is full of questions as she does their hair and dish the ladies the latest but the girls are all guarded about their details. Ah-Donis once again thanks Tasha for the Dolce and Gabanna outfit and the new Versace bag she got her also. Ah-Donis tells her as much.

"Bitch with you back in the hood, a bitch purse can breathe now. For real. Girl so who you and Jazz going to the party with?"

"I'll be with New Jack and she gonna be with Ray Ray". Tasha casually says.

"Wait a minute Bitch, you mean to tell me them two niggas coming to the party boo'd up? Bitch you Ho's pusssies must be lined in gold especially yours. I ain't seen that nigga on lock in forever." Ah-Donis states.

"Things are changing sweetie." Tasha says.

"Bitch Mocha was in here on some boo'd up shit with J-Money and Naomi with Jamaica."

"I really don't know Mocha cause her and my girl Jazz ain't cool and I only see Naomi in passing but it's gonna be OK I hope." Tasha says.

"I don't know, Naomi known to bust heads and Mocha rough too. Now I know I'm gonna be on time to not miss a beat." Ah-Donis says

"Let me get up out of here before it's too late." Was Tasha last words before the girls parted ways.

The girls all kept tabs with the crew as they all went to Spud's to get their heads cut. Each guy had his own swag and outfit to match. Tasha made sure that each one of them had exactly their taste. Ray Ray shelled out the most with wanting some custom Berluti leather pants. Everything else was Bastian and Z Zegna. He bought a new $26,000 pinky ring but tonight wasn't about being flashy cause niggas know he made, it's just a matter of doing big things in front of everyone like the 50,000 he planned to make it rain with.

New Jack is so opposite of Ray Ray. He went all out with Versace and Gucci clothes, a huge necklace and $3000 Alexander Wayne zip up boots.

J-Money just went simple with head to toe Louis Vuitton and a few tasteful but expensive jewels.

Diva's Revenge

Jamaica was the odd ball. He was very specific about what he wanted. He chose a cream thick Hugo Boss sweater and Dior silk pants. Armani on his feet and eyes He was going to wear his custom iced out grill cause he knew that turned Naomi on.

Everyone agreed to meet over Ray Ray's house. The girls met up with Scoop one last time. Scoop told them that this night is very crucial as everyone will be there. When the girls arrived Mocha and Naomi separate, Jazz and Tasha together. They were all surprised to see all of them checking guns. Naomi understood instantly and after a second so did Mocha and Tasha but Jazz had her reservations.

She told Ray Ray that she didn't want to ride in the same car as the guns out of fear of being pulled over. If pulled over she could lose everything. He agreed after a long kiss. They began to look for more for Mocha and J -Money but they were in one of the guest bedrooms. Mocha was giving him oral sex before they left. He was enjoying having his salad tossed and cum drunk before going to the party.

Of course because Tasha and Jazz knew each other, they rode together in the Ghost with New Jack flashy ass and Ray Ray.

Mocha and Naomi wasn't tripping to ride in the Mulsane. Mocha and J- Money exchanged looks and as J-Money grinned she instantly knew the drill and got in the back.

As they put on some Lil Baby and slid down the freeway behind the Ghost, J-Money smoked and pass the blunt to Jamaica and Naomi while Mocha sucked his dick to the beat. When the two most expensive cars arrived at the club it seemed everything and everyone froze. To make matters worse and spark some drama as they arrived, so did Bozo in a Panermera and a couple 750's behind him. New Jack was driving and he dipped in front of Bozo in the line of cars and goes straight to the front of the valet and so does Jamaica. Before words can be exchanged they hop out and make their way to the head of the line without so much as a single word or stop in motion. All eight were ushered into the club.

The owner of Champion ushered them to VIP and the party began. The two largest VIP booths are side by side and as luck would have it, Bozo beat out the niggas from West Dallas and the Nawf to get it. He stepped his game up with that one. As him, Scooter and Melly Mel came by with with Cheetah. Rah Rah, Shanky, Bozo and Ray Ray exchanged a very icy stare.

As the night went on in the club, it got more and more packed, the crew and girls all had fun. All the girls danced except Jazz. She wanted to keep an eye on the surroundings. Slowly everyone in the hood dropped by their table to give props and take pictures with their phones.

As they would upload the pictures to different social medias all of their cell phones would alert them of activity on the sites they have.

Diva's Revenge

A rule in VIP and among other ballers was that you show love by sending a round of shots to their tables for a massive toast. Everyone immediately sent Ray Ray and them a toast except Bozo. Ray Ray had a feeling things would be like this, so he flexed on everyone and ordered shots for the whole club at $150 a shot. Just as the shots started coming around the DJ made the announcement of its source.

All the girls looked at Ray Ray but then they locked eyes with Cheetah, Rah Rah, and Shanky. All night Jazz couldn't put her finger on it but she kept getting a vibe from J-Money and Cheetah. She was constantly eye fucking him and he always danced with Mocha but her back would be to Cheetah and J-Money would be staring at Cheetah.

A big commotion came about when Ah-Donis came in the building. Everybody grabbed her to say hello and take pictures. She is so well known and well respected in the hood that everyone wanted to show her love but she bypassed all that and came straight to Ray Ray and the crew table.

"First off, which one of you bitch's is fucking the owner of the Ghost and who is fucking the owner of the Bentley? Whichever it is you about to have a fight on your hands! Ah-Donis yells over the music

"Shut yo ass up cause you almost there yourself! "New Jack says

"Yeah if she put down the curlers long enough and ride a dick every once in a while!" Ray Ray echoed.

As they are exchanging slugs, they are all talking and taking in what each other have on and taking pictures. All of a sudden, Bozo yells across to her. "Oh yeah Ah-Donis? As much paper my girl and her crew throw your way, you gonna stand over there and act brand new on some weirdo shit!"

"I'm about to make my way over there, boys shut up!" Adonis replied, before anyone knew what was going on.

"Nigga she with hood royalty right now, she'd be over there when we done turning up!" New Jack yells to Bozo.

"You need to stay in your place before your ass come up missing. You know that ain't for us, just keep taking orders to eat nigga. Matter fact did you ask permission from yo master to talk out of turn?"" Bozo said with a smile.

Everyone knew that this is New Jack's element and tonight of all nights was perfect.

"Major Nigga? You are exactly what your name says. A clown ass nigga. You and your lame-ass crew over there driving old ass cars and off the rack clothes. What we drop for the Ghost tonight in yo ho house. We spent more tonight on drinks then you made all month. We major! Just be glad we still letting you eat!" New Jack says.

'Who the fuck you think you talking to? I'll Ray Rice yo ass. You better calm the fuck down!" Scooter says all of sudden.

"Pussy nigga you need to ease up before you be needing some Tylenol up in this bitch!" Jamaica said.

Before things could get any more tense the hood anthem came on and everyone turned up. Ray Ray had decided this will be the perfect time to make it rain.

He grabbed the Goyard duffel bag and Jazz's hand and he and the boys made their way all the way to the dance floor. All eyes were on them as the girls made a circle and started rapping to the song and dancing. Each of the eight all grabbed two handfuls of money and began to make it rain. This came as a surprise to everyone and people didn't know whether to catch the money or record it all.

Bozo stood next to Cheetah with a mean mug on his face. As he was standing there, New Jack gave him and his table the middle finger. He grabs his dick at them also. J-Money starts to dance around in a circle giving them two middle fingers. Next thing you know here comes Melly Mel up in New Jack face.

"Nigga you want to keep breathing in this hood, you put them fingers in Jamaica ass. All you niggas know I don't do no playing. I'll air this bitch out."

Diva's Revenge

"Nigga before I put this finger in yo pussy I'm a put it in yo mama and we will see if you air it out or not. Bitch ass dude fuck you and yo crew I will...."

All hell broke loose when Scooter hit New Jack with a beer bottle. All seven of the niggas started fighting and so did the girls. With all the commotion and so many fighting it took a second for the security to break it up. When they did there was people bleeding, including New Jack, Rah Rah, and Scooter. Everyone gathered their things but the look in Jamaica, J-Money, and RayRay eyes said it was not over.

Once everyone got in the parking lot words were exchanged while they waited on their cars from valet. Scooter made a fatal mistake of saying it's on when his car get here. Ray Ray took out his gun and so did the other three and opened up on him and Melly Mel.

By it being such a huge crowd no one was for sure what happened. But as RayRay, the crew and the girls climbed into the Ghost and the Bentley they knew as they drove past stunned Bozo and a crying Cheetah, Shanky, and Rah Rah. Everyone was silent on the ride home listening to Future and Yo Gotti. RayRay played it all back in his head and he kept saying during all that "where was Bozo at the end?" Everyone on both sides was stunned about the chain of events. As all the cars all fled the scene before the police came, they knew it would all end badly.

Diva's Revenge

When they got back to Ray Ray's place everyone said their goodbyes and left to regroup. On the other side of town, Bozo and Cheetah tried their best to console Rah Rah and Shanky but no one was prepared for Bozo's outlook.

"Where the fuck is the damn police?" Rah Rah screams.

"For what?" Bozo asks.

"Cause J-Money and New Jack bitch ass go pay for this shit." Rah Rah replied

"Damn right these niggas went too far now, I can get a club fight but taking a life?" Shanky says in between tears.

"Fuck the police. We gonna go hold court on these niggas in the streets. When the police get here we gonna all say we don't know who did what, all we know was we got into a fight and things led to shots fired" Bozo said.

"Are you on that shit you sell? These niggas got to go down, fuck wrong with you." Rah Rah yells

"Just Chill and let Bozo Handle it." Cheetah pleads to Shanky and Rah Rah,

"Bitch that's easy for you to say, they didn't kill your man. You gonna be alright when it's all said and done." Rah Rah says.

"That's fucked up Cheetah" Shanky says shaking her head.

"Now you Ho's want to tell me what's fucked up. Bitch if we tell on them its war and they know too much. If we tell the police the truth they gonna look at us closer. We all fired shots too. Think about it." Cheetah says.

"No bitch, you think about it. I can't believe you for real." Rah Rah says

"Man look you Ho's stressing me the fuck out. Look it's like this you can do what you want but I promise you if I get fucked off and I'm unable to handle business I will rock both of y'all to sleep, real talk. What you need to do is chill and let us show you love like the hood does" Bozo exclaimed.

Silence captured everyone as the police pulled onto the scene and began to secure things.

When the girls got home to Jazz's house it was anything but quiet. They had all kinds of things to think about. Things could go wrong real quick. But before long they had it all figured out. It really depended on the hood and how they handled things.

"Okay so I don't know what the fuck just went down but you need to call Uncle Mitch and get him to control the situation. Let him know what really happened and what to do." Tasha tells Jazz.

"I got it, I texted him earlier and he said he would let me back when he knew more." Jazz replied. "I don't know what the fuck these niggas was thinking tonight but I ain't gonna lie, it makes me look at J-Money in a whole new light." Mocha moaned with a smile.

"Girl this shit is most definitely going to get them a bunch of hood credit "Naomi says."

"But what about Bozo? He gonna want to act a donkey and throw his weight around" Jazz said.

"Yeah but he ain't really built like that. He ain't shit without Scooter and Melly Mel. That's why he never tried Ray Ray, cause Ray Ray gonna look at that shit and embarrass him in front of everyone. It's better for people to think you got it and never know. But to be put on the spot niggas would be lining up to take his spot." Naomi says in between puffs of blunt.

"I feel ya! Let's check in with the boys and Scoop and see what's good." says Tasha.

As each girl called and texted the boys on the other side of town at Ray Ray's house a very heated conversation is going on.

"Nigga I knew that yo fucking mouth was gonna start some shit." Ray Ray says while looking at New Jack with disgust.

"Man this shit is outta control. We supposed to be on money and turning up living our best life. Not dodging the police for murder. We already got away once. Y'all go keep pressing y'alls luck?" Jamaica asks.

"Man you niggas act like we asked for them niggas to come sideways. No nigga is gonna play on my top, period. I gives zero fucks who it is and who don't like it. I don't fuck around like that." New Jack declares.

"Ho's explain themselves. I don't have shit to say." J-Money deadpans.

"So, tough ass dudes did you ever think about what could happen to our gals? This could make them all accessory to murder cause they fled with us. My gal is a doctor nigga. Not some jump off thot from the hood." Bozo yells at J-Money and New Jack.

"On top of that, what the fuck! Are you sure any of these Ho's won't fade on us while you putting on capes and shit." J-Money asks.

"It don't matter nigga, we major ass niggas now, doing what we do, we could have dealt with this another way." Says Jamaica.

"So what y'all suggest a nigga do, go back to the scene and turn ourselves in? FUCK OUT OF HERE."

"Keep it up and you go make a nigga go in your 32's." RayRay says.

"Nigga it's yo fault we beefing with the nigga in the first place. You should be really thanking a nigga." New Jack says.

"Yeah with the head of my dick. I don't need no nigga plexing for me. The only thing that might save us is that I been around Bozo enough to know that he sticks to the code of the streets. He gone keep it hood, but trust me the nigga is gonna have to be dealt with in due time. He outnumbered though, so he may come at us in a different form. We will see, but know this, you niggas are my boys and we been through too much to fold now. The hood is ours, buckle up, and now call yo bitches cause Jazz been blowing me up. Let them know we good." Ray Ray tells them before picking up their phones.

At the scene of the Champion Lounge .....

"Sgt Davis. We have two killed by gunshot wounds by two different shooters. No one knows exactly who done it. The victim's families are standing over there." the officer tells Mitch.

"I'll take it from here till crime scene comes." Mitch replies.

In the back of Mitch mind he is replaying Jazz's text and call. Hopefully Bozo and these hood rats won't press the issue. But I raised all of them and feel I can handle it.

"So what happened here?" Mitch asks.

"Shid we had a little scuffle in the club and when we came outside shots were fired." Bozo says looking Mitch in the eye.

"Is that right young ladies?" Mitch asks Rah Rah, Cheetah, and Shanky.

Shanky was rubbing Rah Rah shoulders. Rah Rah raised her head to look at him and instantly Mitch got a bad feeling.

"Mr. Mitch you got to fucking get these bastards. I only want you on the case" She said. In hood terms, she wanted it brushed aside while they do their thing. He looked at her and replied the only thing he knew to.

"Rashonda, I got you. I will personally look into the matter. Just be patient."

"Well if you don't need us Mitch we bout to go, it's been a long night." Rah Rah says.

"Y'all good. I know how to get at y'all if I need anything else." As they were leaving, they all were in a daze as they watched the body bags go into the ambulance.

Mitch watched them leave but before they could get out the parking lot, Bozo backed up as if he forgot something when he seen crackhead Denise approach. Bozo called her to his car and before I knew she had a smile on her face. She whispered something in his ear and the look on his face was not good. Soon, after the car sped away. Mitch was tempted to go ask Denise what was up, but passed.

In Bozo car...

I can't believe this shit. This can't be. If what this bitch Deniece just said is true, this will destroy RayRay faster than any bullet will. I'm about to text this number she gave me to see if it's true. If what I text gets the response I want, it's game over for them. So he texted the crushing text that will change everyone life.

Yeah you grimy bitches, Denise told me yo secret. I know and y'all will pay for what I know.

Whispers....

For the next few days around the hood it was like everyone was whispering about the big night at Champion Lounge. It was so many stories flying around that even Mama Vi had to call a few people to find out what was true or not.

"Hey Mitch, I know you ain't heard from me in a while but I'm okay." Mama Vi says.

"Yeah I thought you were still mad at me about Tanesha." Mitch replied.

"It took me a while but I had to learn to accept fate. This was Tanesha's."

"No, now you making allowances for wrong. No, those bastards day is coming trust me." Mitch assures Mama Vi. "How these same pieces of shits just got away with two more murders all under your watch?" Mama Vi exclaimed.

This stung Mitch and in light of the events, she had a valid point. He just wished he could tell her everything that's going on. For a woman dealing with so much I know it bothers her with all the things around her that seem unfair and unjust. But I promise she will be good in the long run. She just needs to be patient. So he said the only thing he could think of to make her feel at ease.

"Mama Vi they are trying to nail them but without a positive ID or weapon they are squeaky clean. On top of that, we keep hearing different reasons for the incident. But trust me I am on top of it. Mitch stated.

"Well maybe someone in the hood will take the law into they own hands for once. I hope that pussy Bozo finally man up!"

"Mama Vi you have too much pent up anger. Have you been to church?"

"Get off my phone with that shit." Mama Vi slammed the phone down and picked up a cigarette to calm her nerves. He talked like he on their side or some shit.

Meanwhile....

".......Nigga you know shit is about to really be off the chain. New Jack and his crew done smoked Scooter and Melly Mel. Niggas money so long they paid to make shit go away. They say the niggas came to the big party at Champion in a Ghost and Bentley. Only nigga on that level is Mexicans, that nigga Jesse out the west and that fool out the Nawf. I wonder how we gon eat now?"

"Shid nigga I'm go get on my best shit and fuck with them niggas. I been knowing them cause my big bro went to school with New Jack and them..."

"Nigga, them niggas not bout to fuck with you. I'm go try to go through that bitch Naomi. She is on it too. And she fucks with them niggas real tight."

"Good luck, that ho is more rough than all them put together."

Meanwhile....

"..... Yeah that nigga Bozo is due to get robbed. He was ready after Ray Ray left his ass, but now with Scooter and Mel gone, what the fuck is left. This can be an easy come up."

"Nigga that nigga play with them pistols and he don't travel heavy. You go lose your life for some pocket change to that nigga."

"Well what you think we should do?"

"Shid nothing cause something tells me the hood is about to be on fire."

Meanwhile....

".....I can't understand how these niggas kill two niggas in front of everybody and they still walking around."

"What you think we can blackmail the niggas? Tell them that we know they done it and we gone turn state on they ass. It could be at least worth two keys."

"Hell no them niggas will kill you and keep it moving."

"Haven't you heard that nigga J-Money fucking a police detective. How you think they got off that Tanesha shit?"

"Man no way."

"You'd be surprised what money can buy."

Diva's Revenge

"I'll believe it when I see it."

Meanwhile...

"Girl them niggas is certified now. A bitch thought Jamaica was playing for the other team but he with that bitch Naomi and they say he smoked Scooter."

"Bitch I know all them niggas like pussy, cause when I worked at Crybaby's all of them got at me and they all seemed real familiar with pussy."

"Girl you don't know, you stay high, and you don't even know who yo baby daddy!"

Meanwhile....

"......I knew one day this grimy bitch would show her true colors." Rah Rah thought. "I should have listened to my mama when she told me, once you and a ho get into it over a man y'all will NEVER be cool." But Rah Rah always felt that Cheetah had her back. Yea they fought over Maceo way back but since they got to know each other through Shanky it was like a sister bond. Nothing could come between them. They done ran game on niggas and all that. As far as to the point of all being on section 8 housing and juicing niggas to think they paid regular rent. Cheetah was always the one that was for petty schemes. I wanted to be a dope bitch.

Diva's Revenge

When I cut into Melly Mel I thought I had finally snagged a boss nigga. He played it like he was it too. So naturally I introduced Cheetah to Bozo and Shanky to Scooter. But I became so hot and pissed when I found out it was Bozo that was the man.

My mama use to always tell my dad about Bozo but somehow I thought the tide had changed and Melly Mel was the man. He was the one I always saw doing big shit. I thought he was like New Jack, but I was wrong. I kept telling Mel we need to branch out and start fucking with the Jamaicans my mama knows but he was stuck on Bozo. See he was not smart like that nigga Ray Ray was but now his life is gone because of a stupid beef.

Now I have to figure out how to make the most of this awful situation. Things are about to change and when they do I need to be on the up side of things. I don't know what Shanky gon do, she has three kids, and two by Scooter and from what the streets are saying it's like no one even gives a damn about our loss. Bozo says he got it but he all about himself.

On the other side of town....

"........Okay so you think these niggas is ready for fifty keys, when all this shit is going on Naomi?" Magic asks.

"Yeah because the way we all figure it, Bozo is no longer a problem and the niggas in the Nawf and West know better.

Diva's Revenge

We tryna clamp down the hood for good. These niggas need to stack that paper for when we do our thang. It's gonna be like a new version of recycling!" Naomi said.

"Okay I got you now, what's up with us? I need to see you to fuck the shit out of you. As a matter of fact send me some pictures to get me crunk. I ain't had none of that seizure head in over a week. You playing yo role with this clown Jamaica too good. That's my pussy right?" Magic demands to know.

"Boy you know this is all yours. It's just with them smoking Scoot, and Mel. Then the shit with the cluckers, I been having to play clean up. Nigga you know that this shit is all yours." Naomi purrs to him.

"Yeah tell me anything. We will see tonight when I drop off. I'm gonna see how you handle when I long dick you. Daddy will be able to tell from that fosho." Magic says.

"Whatever, I'm about to go so I can get ready." Naomi deadpans.

"Aight" Magic ends.

Naomi gets off the phone and texts her boo a simple message. 'You got 10 minutes to come get this good, I'm horny for real'. She laughed to herself as she laid back in her bed and smoked a blunt watching all the reality shows. If only these niggas knew.

Over the next couple of weeks it seemed it all settled down. No one saw or heard a word from Bozo. All the boys *worked the fifty keys from Magic and all his girls played their parts.*

Word eventually got around the hood that Denise and Fancy caught it trying to rob someone. No one even gave their deaths a second thought. Mobbing in the hood we would see Rah Rah, Shanky, and Cheetah but they kept it moving. They made it a point not to be at Ah-Donis shop where the girls came through. Now that the hood knew they were with the boys. They took turns popping up together but never all four. Tasha would be there more than others because she has business up there.

The boys were now treated like true hood royalty at Spud's as well as in the hood. Jazz and Ray Ray had a few words because he was at that point where he wants to move in together and doesn't want her to work anymore. Of course she's not going to do that because her job is very important to all this. She doesn't want to move in together 'cause he will be able to know all her personal information even though he pays all her bills, it's only so much that he knows.

Tasha and New Jack are okay because she not serious with him, she could care less that he be on dating sites and who he has as friends on social media. She thinks it's cute that he does all this thinking that his game is that tight. She has been having reverse GPS on his phone since day one. It's like she has a clone of his phone. All the girls do. He gives her so much money to the point of her not having to hustle as much but she do it to maintain the girls looks and the boys too. Also some of her faithful clients. Part of her knows that the hustlers is just embedded in her to be a "go getter bitch" plus she has to stay on point!

Mocha is completely opposite of Jazz and Tasha. She loved to sit back and let J-Money take care of her. He refused to allow her to strip anymore. To play the role Mocha had to put up a fight but gave in when he threatened to leave her. He made sure she want for nothing. It really is surprising Mocha that he is spoiling her the way he is but part of that comes from her oral sex game.

She keeps him drain and on flat. He gets it even when he doesn't want it. She shows up unannounced to the spot just to give him oral sex. But the key is to never let him know he matters she didn't bug him or ask crazy ask questions. She just chilled and played her position as a boss bitch. They been going to the Audi dealership looking at cars but if he knew that she beyond that.

Naomi is like a gangster's dream. She is ready at every turn for whatever but she also has incredible insight thanks to Scoop. She is always, it seems, two steps ahead of how Jamaica thinks and it fucks his head up. She is down on the sex game and money game too! She has saved him on a couple potential fuck ups. Because Scoop keeps his ear to the street, he knew the grimy *sheet that was about to happen and she was able to avoid it smoothly.*

This has put her as an equal with all the boys. They all talk to her on a regular basis and all are close to her. In due time she and the girls plan to use that to their advantage. But it was something that Jamaica did a couple weeks ago that has been in the back of Naomi's mind for some reason.

He surprised her with a huge bottle of Miss Dior but everyone knows that Marc Jacobs's scents are my favorite and Dior is Mocha's favorite scent. Every time you see her, she has it on. Maybe he smelled it on her one day and wanted me to have it but what stuck in my mind is him saying baby, "I got your favorite smell good." To this day I can't get this nagging feeling out my head. Oh well, he's not my man, Magic is, so what the hell.

Diva's Revenge

Chapter 7: They Got To Go!

The girls' mood was subdued as they talked and waited on Uncle Mitch to come. This meeting had a lot of things that needed to be fixed because if they wasn't careful things could spiral out of control really quick. The girls all wondered exactly what Bozo knew, but it had to be big because he said he knew all of our secrets. That could mean a lot and fuck up the whole plan.

Each girl went through a lot to keep things under wraps but there was an obstacle. Uncle Mitch texted Jazz and told us that we all needed to meet. When he came in his face was full of conviction and he wasted no time lighting into our asses.

"Why the fuck did none of you try to stop Jamaica, New Jack, Ray Ray and J-Money?" asked Mitch.

"Honestly we didn't know shit was about to pop off." replied Tasha.

"I take the blame because I should have put my foot down when I first saw they were carrying guns." yelled Jazz.

"Girl them niggas gonna do what they want. We just have to stick to the plan. Hopefully Uncle Mitch cleaned it up for us." Naomi says.

"You damn right I cleaned this shit up. I can't have my niece tied up in this shit. It was people at the party saying they saw all y'all shooting guns so my mission was to contain it all and chalk it up as a hood beef thing. Now when I talked to Bozo he went out his way to let me know they didn't see shit and don't know shit. Rashonda was all upset screaming about justice but we can handle her when the time comes." Uncle Mitch declares.

"So now that we are clear on all that we now need to talk about what to do about these grimy ass bitches Denise and Fancy. Bozo knows something from them and in due time we will all find out but we need to deal with them before they keep talking." Mocha says.

"I'm down. I ain't liked them Ho's since they sold me bogus Home Depot gift cards. Fuck them Ho's. I would do the shit myself." Naomi exclaims.

"No I have the perfect situation for them it's just about timing and all. Besides, they just two hood crackheads, no one is going to even blink if they come up missing or somewhere stanky. Now the question is disappearance of them or found "stanky" as a message. Uncle Mitch asked.

Everyone came to the conclusion to send a message and leave them in the hood at a known spot for Bozo. It could kill two birds with one stone for them, shut up Bozo 'cause he will be too busy trying to get the blame off him. They would time it when Bozo is the last one seen talking to them two.

Another matter that needed to be talked upon was sex. Originally the girls said they were going to string them along but as each talked it was becoming clear that none of them had adhered to this, especially Mocha and Tasha.

Naomi is doing double duty and expresses that she enjoys sex with Jamaica. He is a freak like she likes him and has no hang ups about pleasing her. Jazz then shocks everyone by telling how Ray Ray is weird and likes to do it with the lights on. She plays it off 'cause he so ugly there she can only enjoy it riding him backwards. All of the girls say that a lot of times they get by with only oral sex. Mocha says J-Money can't get enough of it. They just all hope that none of them starts talking about kids. That is not any of the girls plans They can't stand none of those dudes, let alone have kids with them.

So Uncle Mitch in between laughing and warnings finishes the meeting and leaves to set things in motion. As he is about to leave, he bypassed Scoop on his way into the house to meet with the girls. Scoop tells us what we already know but he adds a few nuggets that we didn't. From what Scoop tells us Bozo is preparing to take Ray Ray and them down but he says he not gonna do it with pistol play he gonna use their girls.

Diva's Revenge

Now we know Bozo's days are very much numbered. He is starting to pose more of a threat to the girls than the niggas and they couldn't have that. Scoop is eager to do the fool 'cause no one would suspect him but Tasha and Jazz makes sense by saying wait and let things simmer down from the party. He reluctantly agrees but still feels it's time to remove him off the chess board.

Two days later....

Ever since Denise gave Bozo that info, he has been giving them blessings when he sees them around. Little did he know that Denise and Fancy has started making it their business to see him often. Every now and then Fancy would give Bozo some head for extra work. It was this situation that proves to be Bozo's downfall.

He was in one of his duck off cars that no one really knew about and while Denise was in the back seat, Bozo got head from Fancy. While in the midst of Denise smoking and Fancy blowing Bozo wig back no one saw the gunman creep up on the Toyota Corolla and dump the silenced bullets in Denise and Fancy. Through the shattered window the gunman threw a small note. Bozo first looked around to see if anyone was looking.

SNAP SNAP SNAP SNAP

He couldn't have seen Uncle Mitch in the wing snapping pictures. As Bozo read the letter with three words on it, he regained his composure and did what his gut was telling him to do. He ate the piece of paper that said

YOU NEXT BITCH

Next he looked around for anybody that just so happened to be walking around. Once he saw no one was in the vicinity he pushed both bodies out of his car and got the fuck out of there. This could mean a lot of shit in a lot of ways. He didn't know what angle all this could come from.

Everyone saw him talking to the police at the party but then there was Tasha and her crew, but why would these bitches want to kill me for knowing that they know each other? I mean when I text the number that that snake ass Denise gave me, all I got was a "who is this" response. I know shit is getting real fucked up around the hood real quick. It's too much shit happening that no one can explain I need to figure it out before it's too late.

Meanwhile....

"......Yeah I took care of both Denise and Fancy. I got pictures to shut Bozo's ass up. As we speak I'm on my way to show and tell with him." Uncle Mitch tells an excited Jazz.

"Okay I will pass the word on to the girls. This takes a lot of pressure off and lets us get back towards the focus." Jazz states.

"Now that's what the fuck I want to hear, 'cause for a minute y'all started to get all caught up in shit. I'm having to step in too often and too early. This is what Scoop is supposed to be doing. Uncle Mitch vents.

"I know and I promise from this point on things will go a lot smoother for us. Now it's time to start throwing around our weight." says Jazz.

"Look I don't care how you handle it, all I want is for them to eventually pay and know why, so I can tell Mama Vi and set an example of what will not be ever again tolerated period. Now let me go so I can pick up Armand.

Chapter 8: "Do what?"

Since the party, after everything settled down, the boys all started a routine of getting together on Sundays to watch the game. Normally it would be held at Ray Ray's house. This was cool with the girls 'cause they all didn't want their homes to be up for a choice. They wanted it to remain that they met the boys on their turf. Yeah, true enough each dude has been to the girl's house, but no one wanted to make it a habit.

Things couldn't have fallen into play on a better note. New Jack and Tasha texted everyone and said that this Sunday New Jack was hosting things at his crib. They were going all out. New Jack, the one that always likes to be flashy, wanted a chance to show off the new home theater system he just got. So he felt the time had come to do so. The girls talked it over with Scoop and he felt it was time to create some tension.

Jazz wanted to continue to play it as her and Tasha are the only ones that are cool. Naomi and Mocha are semi alright. They wanted to keep up this plan as separate in order to individually work the boys. When Jazz, Mocha and Naomi called Tasha to ask if they needed to bring anything they were all told "no". Tasha explained that this was New Jack first time having a lot of his family over to meet her. So it was best that the girls do their best for them. At first the girls were nervous about the plan but Tasha said it would be okay and things should go off without a hitch.

When they all showed up with their boys, they immediately saw that things were in full swing. New Jack's family was what you would call on the borderline of being 'soulful in the hood'. They did all the cliche things that people do in the hood, but they were all on point thanks to Tasha. They had card games and Domino's going on in his backyard and everyone else was inside his house watching the games. Everyone said their hellos and Tasha looked beautiful in a cream and red DVF dress. Tasha and Jazz mostly talked and Naomi talked to everyone. Mocha kinda stayed to herself when she wasn't talking to J-Money. The family all seemed to love Tasha and the girls. A few of them knew the girls from Ah-Donis shop or from just being around the way in the hood.

One of the girls made a comment about the Jamaica and Tanesha incident but everyone brushed it off when looking at Naomi. She was so sexy in her all white Burberry. The girls took turns snuggling up to the boys and taking pictures for social media as well as for personal keep. During taking these pictures Jazz used that as the perfect time to go with the plan. While everyone was posing for pictures Jazz began to frown towards Mocha. It became so apparent that Ray Ray stopped and asked what's wrong. This led to all hell breaking loose quick.

"Nothing it's just this bitch keep fucking up all the pictures posing like a prostitute and shit!" Jazz says. "Who baby?" Ray Ray asked although he didn't want to know 'cause he knew it was gonna be drama.

Pointing, Jazz looked at Mocha who had a surprised look on her face.

"Bitch don't hate 'cause I'm eye candy." Mocha exclaimed.

"What I need to hate for, look at me!"

"Yeah I know, that's why I know it's hate. You dumb Ho's kill me wanting smoke with a boss bitch for fame." Mocha says and laugh.

"Bitch I'm a doctor with a degree, last time I checked Harvard doesn't offer degree plans for sliding down a pole. Can you even spell Harvard? Are you smarter than a fifth grader?" Jazz says.

"Okay y'all don't do this right now. Y'all know how important today was for New Jack." Tasha pleas.

"Girl shut yo fat ass up. Nobody even talking to you. You can get the slap this bitch about to get." Mocha screams.

"Bitch all that pole dancing got you on some dumb dumb shit. Don't let the degree fool you I'll beat a bitch up in here." Jazz says smoothly.

By now all the boys are gathering and trying to stop things from getting out of hand. While everyone is talking to Jazz, Mocha reaches across and slaps Jazz. When Jazz recovered from the slap she made one statement to let everyone know how mad she was.

"If you motherfuckers keep holding me, when I get loose I'm going to give you the leftovers of the ass whooping this bitch about to get!" Ray Ray then yells for everyone to let her go.

"Ya'll got me fucked up if ya'll think y'all go hold her while this ho swing off on her. Let my bitch get her round. Nigga don't like it we can look at that shit."

With this said everyone moved out of the way and Jazz and Mocha went at it. Mostly they pulled hair and got a couple of body kicks and punches. Everyone eyebrows went up when they fell on the floor. After a few moments Ray Ray and J-Money both pulled the girls apart. Both girls were still firing off slugs at each other about the other.

When Ray Ray tried to console Jazz she stormed to her car and left. So did Mocha. When both girls were up the street they met at the gas station and laughed and hugged while they looked at the text and calls coming in from everyone. They told Scoop what went down and he also got a good laugh out of it.

Diva's Revenge

Jazz texted Ray Ray and expressed that she didn't care to be in company of any of them except Tasha and New Jack. She texted New Jack and Tasha and gave a fake apology. Mocha echoed all of these actions with J-Money but unlike Ray Ray who wanted to give Jazz space to vent and chill, J-Money demanded to know where Mocha was so he could come through and be with her. She played it off like she was okay and would catch up with him later. Naomi and Jamaica left. They both were drained from the whole thing and needed to regroup.

A couple hours later all the girls made up with Scoop. Everyone took turns filling him in on the events at New Jack's house. They all got a good laugh out of it. The whole time they were telling the stories of the boy's reactions they were all getting text from them. None of the girls notice until Tasha brought it up that a complete hour went by and none of the boys hit them up. They didn't really care 'cause they were laughing and having a good time with Scoop.

While the girls were all smiles, across town in New Jack's house it was anything but that. Ray Ray and J-Money were having words and it seemed things were about to get out of hand.

"You bring another one of yo uppity bitches around with her stank ass attitude and you expect the real hood bitch not to check her? I'm surprised Naomi didn't smash yo ho sooner." J-Money says to Ray Ray.

"Nigga it's you fucking up bringing this rat around all this cheese. I thought the rules don't save' em?" Ray Ray said.

"My girl cuts for both y'all gals, she don't have a problem. She just on money and my dick. Bypass her with all the misdemeanor and shit." Jamaica laughs and says.

"I think all ya'll owe me and Tasha an apology. She went all out for this day for me and she ain't did nothing but show all y'all love since she started kicking it with me." New Jack looks at everyone and says.

"Nigga you trippin. I'm a gangsta. I don't do no apologizing and I'm especially not going to for my girl smashing on an uppity ho." J-Money declares.

"One more time and we will test all that shit you talking about. Look I'll bust...."

Before it could go any further New Jack and Jamaica jumped in between them and became the voice of reason. After a brief intense standoff both of them decided to leave and cool off. Once they left Jamaica and New Jack had a long talk and came to some needed conclusions about things.

Ray Ray left to find Jazz and let her know that he has her back. But what Ray Ray and the rest didn't know was things were about to heat up for them.

Diva's Revenge

Later.....

Ray Ray and Jazz were laying in bed together and Jazz asked him a question that somewhere Tasha, Mocha and Naomi would all be echoing soon.

"What do you see in us? I mean I am enjoying our relationship but Ray Ray I'm at that age where I need to start making a life and building my future. You feel me?" Jazz asked him.

"Damn baby what are you trying to say? You want to move on and do something different?"

"Look I'm going to be honest with you. A couple of days ago my college roommate called me crying. She, too, fell in love with a hood nigga. Well he had a bunch of things like you do, but when he got hit, they took it all and now all she has is the clothes on her back. I loaned her a large amount of money and I'm giving her my old Maxima I had in college. But what I'm saying is if we gonna be doing this we have to plan better.

I have excellent credit and we could put things in my name. Really I feel like all of y'all are at a point with y'all gals to put things in their name. I don't really know J-Money and Jamaica situation, but I know you and New Jack should do it. I mean I'm not going anywhere and at this point I have just as much to lose as you, I just don't..."

"You don't have to sell it to me baby girl, actually me and New Jack been on this page. We need to spring it on J-Money and Jamaica but you are right. We work too hard to let it all get taken so easily. I'm down. Let me get at them about it." Ray Ray says.

All the girls, except Mocha, had the same conversation with the boys and they all, yet reluctantly, agreed that this is the best course of action. Everyone had their own reservations about the others.

A week later...

Ray Ray called all them over to his house and told them to bring their girl with them. Once everyone got there Ray Ray made apologies for the fight at New Jack's house. He apologized for everyone 'cause he knew no one would do it first. Moving along he told the crew about the situation they were in with making as much money as they do. He talked about how he worked too hard to get to where they are and how it would hurt them to take any losses right now. At first J-Money thought he was talking about getting robbed and he spoke up on the perimeters that they have taken.

Ray Ray said he wasn't taking about that and he then talked about going a step further to make sure that if the Feds started looking at them, they will be good. Ray Ray told them that with the stuff with Bozo and them killing Scooter and Melly Mel, you never know who could be looking at them. It's just better to be on point for when it does happen. He gave examples of a few cats in the hood that took major hits from not being prepared well enough. Finally J-Money just straight out asked Ray Ray what's the business.

"Man what the fuck is you trying to say?" J-Money asked.

"Man we need to start putting our stuff in other names besides ours. Right now we got too much in our names to be safe." Ray Ray replied.

"I mean I could use my grandma or Mama but neither one of them got jobs." J-Money said.

"Naw I'm talking about our girls." Ray Ray shot back.

"Do what? Nigga I know you on some more shit. I barely trust a bitch with twenty to go get cigars, let alone give up control over all I got. Yeah, okay, good luck with that." J-Money sarcastically laughs and shakes his head.

"I'm down. Tasha is the only bitch I'm even fucking with right now. Plus she got her own shit, she don't need mine, real talk." New Jack exclaims.

"Same thing with Naomi. She ain't did shit but brought to the table since we've been together. I trust her with my life. We've been knowing her forever." Jamaica said.

Everyone turned to look at J-Money. He set back with a frown on his face and puffed on the blunt. Mocha knew he would be this way but it still kind of hurt to see all the other girls niggas down and he wasn't. So she decided to try her luck and see what's up.

"First off you niggas to sit here and talk about this as if we not here. OK, it's like this. I don't know Tasha or Jazz and I really don't know Naomi that well but I can say that since I have been with you J-Money and saw the impact that us as a unit have had, I feel that everyone here has each other's best interest at heart. Me and Jazz had our differences but I'm here for you. I feel anything I need to do, I'll do it. You don't trust me but you want me to give up how I make a living on the faith of you? Is that fair?" Mocha crossed her arms and looked at him.

"She do got a point on that. I mean you did tell me you didn't want her stripping if she was gonna be your gal." Jamaica said.

"What the fuck is this? Gang up on J-Money or some shit. Y'all so trusting put y'all shit in ya girls' name. I'm good." J-Money said.

Silence fell over the room. Mocha quietly got up and left the house. Shortly after so did J-Money. Everyone else talked of all the pros and cons. Then they all branched off with their dudes and regrouped. Tasha and New Jack sat for hours at the park and talked about how to do things. He wasn't worried about all that stuff J-Money was talking about. Everyone knew that he was super paranoid and overdid it when it came to business.

Diva's Revenge

His gut has saved us a couple times but New Jack felt that Mocha was a good girl and J-Money might have ran her away. He and Tasha talked about it and Tasha let him know that she wished she could do more but they not cool. It was on him and the boys to get in J –Money's ear.

Naomi and Jamaica went to eat at the hood hotspot and afterwards they went back to Naomi's spot. They reached the agreement that in the morning they would go transfer everything to Naomi. When she texted Scoop with the news, he immediately texted back that that was not a good idea 'cause then he could find out her real information on all her cars and homes. She needed to figure out how to do it without him. She could call him from a lawyer's office and do it that way but he does not need to be present.

Ray Ray and Jazz took a whole different approach about it. They got on the Internet and looked at all the legal sites that walk you through how to do it. They both called Naomi, Tasha, New Jack and Jamaica and told them about what they found. When all of them heard of how easy it was, the girls told the boys that they would find a lawyer that all of them could go to to do all the paperwork. Little did the boys know that the lawyer that they were using was Uncle Mitch's lover Armand.

Over the next week the girls got a true glimpse at what all the boys had in their possession. It really shocked them but they all played it cool. At the same time, Ray Ray decided to show them the stash house in Pleasant Grove that he thought they didn't know about. With all this going on, they all became real close.

No one saw Mocha but the girls all kept in touch and told her that she was doing good. J-Money tried to put up a good front but everyone could tell that he missed Mocha. Mocha said that he would send her dumb text asking if she has certain items of his over at her house or in the car. She would give a very short NO response and keep it moving. One night he called her drunk and said a few things. Scoop says he don't be in no Ho's faces in the hood and the girls says he never bring anyone over, so now it was really a waiting game to see if he gets his mind right.

Two weeks later.....

Tasha called Mocha and told Mocha that it was time to "drop by" where J-Money was. Tasha told her to put on that white BCBG highwaisted skirt and black and white leather Tom Ford top. Come over and look like a million bucks. She went to Ah-Donis earlier that day so her hair was on point. She pretended to be in the area and came by to get some things Tasha had for her. When Tasha told J-Money she was on her way and was 10 minutes away, he lit up and started pacing, waiting to see her.

When she walked in the door and saw him she pretended to be disgusted at the sight of him. When she attempted to brush past him, he grabbed her arm.

"Look don't be grabbing on me as if we on that level." Mocha said while she glared at his hands on her.

"Man why you acting like that? You know how I...."

"Know what? It's clear I don't know a bitchass thang. Listen last time you got to do all the talking now it's my turn. Nigga if I was on some grimy shit I coulda been set you up. You forgot I'm with you all the time. I'm not the one suggested putting shit in my name, it was YO PEOPLE. I don't need you for shit. I'm with you 'cause I want to be. Don't EVER feel that you got it like that. I'm a good bitch, any nigga will be happy to have me." Mocha said.

"I know this Mocha. Let me try to say this right. I want you by my side as my bitch, you make a nigga happy, you keep a nigga drained and I don't feel no slick shit from you. It just all caught me off guard."

"So what now?" Mocha asked.

"I want you in my life. I want the shit that my niggas now got. A piece of mind. I don't want to keep looking over my shoulder." J-Money said.

"OK...." Mocha says.

"Why the fuck you making this shit weird being all corny and shit as fuck." Yells J-Money.'

"Cause I am a woman and that's what we do." Mocha laughs.

"Girl is we go get with Ray Ray and New Jack and do things like they did it?"

He then pulled her close and they kissed for a very long time. Then they snuck off and did what they always do. She pleased him with her mouth 'cause he was long overdue. They told Tasha and Ray Ray they were leaving and they went to his house.

That night Tasha and Mocha texted and set up to meet the next day. J-Money talked to Ray Ray before he left and he gave him the number for the lawyer. Although he had a bunch of fears about doing it, the next day he and Mocha met with Armand and he reluctantly transferred all his things to Mocha. The original transfers were bogus and later Armand and the girls did the real transfer.

Chapter 9: Scoop

My name is Scoop to everyone in the hood. Outside of that no one can really tell you anything important about me. They don't know my real name, where I live or if I have a wife and kids. But everyone in the hood trusts me. I came to the hood 6 years ago and started working my way into the hood.

I did all the grunt work that all the other crackheads in the hood charged to do. I went out my way and eventually became cool with the stores in the hood where they would let me clean up for them. Most niggas in the hood don't want to leave their spot since it gets to going on a hot night, so I am the runner that goes and gets them food, cigars and drinks. All I ask for is the crumbs sometimes. But no one in the hood ever see me smoke. I am sometimes so invisible that a lot of people pay me no mind and do business in front of me.

I worked extremely hard to be invisible to them cause I wanted to be able to soak up all the information I could on four hood niggas in particular. For the past six years I have watched their every move. I know what they all do and don't like. I know the kind of females they go for, all the way down to what they like to wear and where they all live.

While I gathered this information, I passed it along to my girls to build themselves up for the takedown. If these niggas knew who I really was, it would fuck they heads up that I am this close to them. It was chance that I came upon the girls. One day I was being invisible in the hood and Naomi was talking on her phone to her girls about these same cats. But from what they were planning I knew it could get real messy and blown out of proportions.

So I set it up for me to meet them myself. Once I gave Naomi a rundown of all I knew she immediately wanted to introduce me to her friends. In all my years I have never seen a crew of bitches that so lethal. The potential within them is so scary but they needed direction. I knew their secret and it all works for me.

Through me the girls are able to have eyes and ears in the streets. It's impossible for them to be in the hood in the capacity that they need to without drawing attention. So that's where I am key, but I needed them to get close to the niggas in order to access certain stuff. Uncle Mitch plays a major role too as cleanup for us. Everyone never stops to think why they only see me on certain days and only certain hours. I go home. Yes I have a home. Actually I have more than one but I like for them to believe that

I'm a bum with nothing. I wear the same three outfits all the time and I rarely run with anyone.

But I see and know everyone in the hood. I know what they have and who they run with. I even know a lot of grimy shit that niggas do behind each other's back. Because of this, I knew that finding niggas to do what I needed done was out of the question. You can only rule a real man for so long before his leadership kick in. And if a nigga allows himself to be ruled for too long, you really should be afraid of him, he could prove to be deadly.

Growing up in the hood, I always was the standout that strived to be above the rest in whatever I did. And at this point I'm the best because I'm steps ahead of a lot of niggas. I have what most niggas lack in life, I have patience, discipline and determination in me.

It amazes me that no one ever sat and wondered why I never went with Fast Black and Carwash Mike to hit licks for money and I stuck to what I do. Most crackheads get greedy and want more but I remain content with my crumbs. It was like a recycling bin in a lot of ways.

If they only knew how close me and Naomi was. How she wind up getting under my skin is still a mystery. I think I feel for how gangster out of the four she is. She surprised me with some of the shit coming out her mouth.

Diva's Revenge

Overall I'm happy with all of them and I like how our strategy is coming all together. When it's all said and done, I plan to shock the hood and leave a mark that no one will believe. This shit me and my girls is doing is shit legends are made of. Although I wear the same three outfits they are extremely expensive. Each of the three pair of pants I wear are all European brands that start at 600 or better. So are the shirts. But the shades that are my signature are low key Cartier that cost $2500.

I wanted them extra dark because they hide my eyes and you are never able to know what I'm looking at. I smeared this stuff that they use in movies over my teeth to make them look rotted but underneath is a set of veneers that cost well over $50,000. My very comfortable shoes are Berluti resort wear. I keep on a hat because I don't want them to see my well-groomed haircut.

I go to extreme measures for my looks to come across as a bum but I'm not and very soon the hood will know.

Chapter 10: Car Trouble

It seems like ever since the girls gained control of the boy's stuff it's almost like they are married now. I mean now they want to be around the girls all the time. In a lot of ways this is what the girls all wanted, but at times it could be taxing. Before they put the boys stuff in their names, they thought they knew all of them but now even Scoop couldn't have prepared them for what came next.

This is especially true for J-Money. He was constantly around Mocha and now he's to the point where he now questions where she's been. Of course, at first she thought it was funny and adorable but now it was getting on her nerves. For a girl that always played by her own rules, she couldn't really adapt to all that noise. But she knew she had to keep her cool.

Even though he's being real jealous and possessive, all of that almost went out the window the other day while they were riding in the car. J-Money had woke her up early that morning with a phone call telling her that he was up the street. It made her alarmed 'cause she liked to be on point when she saw him. His call was brief but very romantic.

"Hey sleepyhead, daddy almost there to get you. I want to spend the day with you so get dressed and wear something sexy but comfortable. J-Money said.

"Boy I know yo ass got jokes. I am not about to get up out this bed." Mocha yelled into the phone.

"I'm four exits up from you. I'll just come in and jump on the bed and make a bunch of noise till my sexy lady gets up and goes with me. If that don't work I'm gonna rub my dick across your lips." J-Money says while laughing.

"At least tell me where we going so I'll at least know how to dress." Mocha replied.

"Out to eat, somewhere outdoors then somewhere indoors, all within walking distance of each other." J-Money states.

"OK I gotta go so I can get ready." Mocha jumped up and went to her closet. She quickly grabbed a pair of AG jeans, a vintage YSL T- shirt and some studded over the knee boots. She pulled her hair into a side ponytail and lightly applied makeup and was ready by the time he finally came upstairs and laid in her bed. She smiled at him looking so casual in head to toe True Religion and Balenciaga sneakers on. We headed out the door and jumped in his Benz truck, the whole time laughing and talking.

First we went to run a couple of errands in the far side of town before we started our date. I was slightly annoyed because J-Money could have did all of this before coming to get me. Then it made me smile at the thought of how he was trying to include me in his life, which is a lot for a nigga like him that is so paranoid. After a while I slipped into a silence as we headed to where we were going on the tollway. I was sending texts back and forth with Tasha 'cause she was sending me pictures of stuff she had just got from Atlanta for me and J-Money. At the same time I'm on social media with Jazz while she's at work.

When I looked up, I slightly notice that J-Money has a mask on his face. I thought maybe it's because he seen on social media where a male friend likes my picture from today but after a while I asked him something and his response tells me it's not me. He still used "baby" towards me, and when he made he uses other words or he gets real silent on me. So, I finally had enough and I bite the bait and I asked him what's up.

"Baby what's wrong? Why the ugly faces all of a sudden?"

"Man, it's this lame as nigga at every light, he breaking his neck looking in my truck at you." J-money exclaims.

"Daddy you tripping he might be just checking your truck out. I mean it is killing the game." Mocha replies.

"Four lights? And this nigga keeps mugging me and you. He about to make me dump on his ass with that Ho shit" J -money yells over the music.

Mocha can tell now that he's upset so she tried to take his mind off of it while asking is he still following. She started to feel on his dick and it instantly got hard and she smiled.

"Here this nigga comes again all fast and shit like he trying to catch us." J-Money said.

When they got to the next light Mocha turns to see who it was when they got to the next light. The Lexus pulled up to them.

To Mocha he looked vaguely familiar but not enough to care. J-Money says to her, "You see how he looking at us?

When they pulled over to a gas station so did the Lexus. Before they could even turn off the engine the man in the Lexus was out of his car and at Mocha window with a gun. He started screaming at her. "Bitch you remember me? You thought you got away with this shit, I'm gonna blow your brains out for that shit you nasty bitch. It's Ho's like you they need to line up and kill, you are a sick bitch."

At this point he cocked the gun back and Mocha screamed for J-Money to take off. Just as he was, the man in the Lexus slammed the butt of the gun into Mocha window and shattered it. J-Money took off and once he seen that the Lexus wasn't following, he pulled over to check on Mocha. His face had a mix of expressions, part was fear, part anger and part was full of curiosity. Quietly he and Mocha called the police and also their crew. First to get there was New Jack, at the same time the police did. The whole time J-Money wouldn't look at her or say one word to her.

He told the police that it was road rage and they got away before they could get a plate number. The police took a report and statement for J-Money's insurance company. Once they left he called Ray Ray and told him they were OK and that New Jack was there. During all the chaos neither he nor Mocha noticed that neither of them received responses from Naomi and Jamaica. New Jack asked while on the phone with Tasha if they were OK. Once they said they had it, he left. Mocha couldn't be seen talking on the phone to Jazz since the fight, so she texted her that she was OK and will talk to her later. Mocha turns to J -Money and asked him what was next?

"You mean a nigga runs up on my shit with a gun, shatters my shit and all you can ask is what's next?" J-Money asked in shock.

"I mean I'm sorry for what happened but that's part of my past." Mocha replied.

Mocha knew who he was now, she and Angel had clipped him for money but it was so long ago and she changes her looks so much how did he recognize her?

"So that's all the fuck you got to say, I'm about to have my brains blown out and all you can say is that! Bitch you out of there.

I don't know what the fuck you used to dealing with but that ain't gonna cut it." J-Money yelled at her with his finger in her face.

"Look before I got on at the good clubs, I did some grimy shit to survive on these streets. Fuck yo ass nigga this is coming from the same one that dumped on a nigga at a party in front of me on some mo shit. Miss me with the sentimental ass lame shit." Mocha says in defense while swiping her finger at his face.

"That's different. So how many of these niggas looking for you? Am I gonna have to start back riding with my pistol in my lap when I'm with you? Dayum Mocha!"

"I don't know. I'll pay for your window. Just take me home.

J-Money cleared the glass out the seats and climbed in and went to get the window fixed in complete silence. When they got close to her house, he finally decided to speak. What he said made things all the worse for her.

"Look Mocha your past is your past but you gotta step yo shit up here. I'm not an average nigga. We got too much major shit going on to get fucked off on some minor hoodrat shit. Whatever you clipped that nigga for we spend in one day on one outfit. Think about it get yo shit together before it's too late, I cut for you but I can't rock like that."

He kissed her on the cheek and leaned back in his seat and turned up the music. Normally he will play on this phone till I text him and let him know everything was OK but today when Mocha looked out the corner of her eye before she went in, his truck was already leaving.

Meanwhile...

"..........Oh this is my bump right here. Have you heard the remix with......?"

Before Naomi could finish what she was saying Jamaica had changed the station. At first she thought he was being playful, so she turned it back. Immediately he turned it again. Naomi crossed her arms and looked at him sideways. She waited and finally he spoke

"Look I can't tell you what to bump in your shit, but Frank Ocean gets no air time in my rides. Niggas not turning up to no homo." Jamaica says.

"What the fuck difference does who he with matter. I fucks with his music. You sound lame as fuck."
Naomi replied.

"Look, I know you bitches get all sensitive for these nasty ass fags but I'm a man and we not gonna bump that shit in here. End of subject." Jamaica exclaims and turns up the radio. Naomi sat there for a moment and weighed all her options.

If she did too much it could blow up in her face. The hood bitch in her wanted to regulate this nigga but she had to stay in position. So she did stand firm and bring it to him in another angle. She turned down the music.

"For real, man you gonna fuck a nigga high up. Let me hurry up and drop you off so you can go dance in Cissy land."

"First off let's get one thing overstood today. Respect me and my feelings. I have no problem that you don't like Frank Ocean or any other gays but that's your issue not mine. First and last mistake. If we gonna kick it come to me as an equal, never less! You feel me?" Naomi states.

"Ain't nobody trying to hear that lame ass shit. To solve this problem don't touch my shit at all or don't ride. Plain as that. And don't get shit twisted Boo, we never equals, you here 'cause I want you to be. "Jamaica exclaimed.

Naomi was shocked at this. Part of her felt hurt that he felt this way but she kept in mind that he was mad right now and he's a man and men hate to be challenged. But he had one thing right, they were not equals at all. He has forgotten Naomi owns all his shit. For the remainder of the ride they both said nothing. They were going to eat, but that's out the door. When they got to her house they said nothing as she got out the car. She threw her Chloe bag over her shoulder and walked to her door.

Diva's Revenge

When she looked back and saw he was gone she jumped in her Jag XJ and sped off. She needed to vent and see what to do about him. When she looked down at her phone she saw all the missed calls from Mocha, Tasha and Jazz. She was not prepared for what they told her had happened when she talked to Mocha. They were already all together and it made it easier. So she headed to meet up with all of them. When she got to Mocha's house the girls were all laughing at Mocha's story about the trick she had got back in the day. Naomi had to admit that it was funny now that it was over but they all knew that this was a very serious issue. They talked about how J-Money received this and the other boy's reaction to it.

Ray Ray was cool and made a few good points about being more careful that Jazz relayed to them. Of course New Jack had a 1000 jokes for her and Tasha told most of them to lighten the mood. She gave them the clothes that she had for them. Naomi told them about Jamaica and the Frank Ocean incident. They all told her that that was to be expected 'cause after all the buzz about the Tanesha thing he naturally gonna have a complex about things.

She thought about it for a while as she hit the blunt and after a while she thought better of it. Both her and Mocha texted the boys apologizing and wanting to make up. It took more on Naomi's part because she had to stroke his ego. Both of them was happy to receive the girls. Tasha and Jazz were happy to report that they were doing OK with Ray Ray and New Jack. They called Scoop to check in and let him know what was up.

While he laughed at the details that the girls told him, he also let them know that he heard all of the boys in the hood talking about the different incidents. But they never said anything about leaving the girls. Scoop told them how Ray Ray chastised both of them and let them know that in J-Money case, he had to take those type of issues with the territory. As far as Jamaica he was to the extreme, they talked a bit more about what's next and then they ended the call. The girls all said goodbyes and left. Nobody paid any attention to the gray Impala sitting at the end of the street with Bozo in it.

Chapter 11: Ah-Donnis

The girls hadn't really been around each other since the Mocha incident. The boys had really been up under the girls lately. Really spending time. Now that they were all deeply involved with the boys it was rare that all of them met up to do their rituals. But Tasha would see all of them at different times at Ah-Donis shop. By it being so close to Christmas all the girls said they were going to go in early and get sew-ins. That way, Christmas week all they would need is a touch up. Jazz and Mocha still played their role of not doing each other to the boys but today they were all going to meet up at Ah-Donis for their appointments. As planned, each girl went through their closets to find the dopest outfits, cause Ah-Donis shop is the shit. You never come half stepping at all. As they each went through their closet they also thought back to all the events of recent that they had to catch up on.

Jazz......

These bitches have really been on me about kicking it and I missed them too, but with all the demands from work and Ray Ray, it's hard to find time. But I did make sure that I let them know the business about Ray Ray. Really things have been running itself. We've been kicking it a lot and enjoyed spending time together. Sometimes it be the simplest things like running my bath water or meeting for lunch while I'm at work. I went through my closet and found a nice pair of graphic print leggings and a cute Marc Jacobs motorcycle jacket to go with her simple Beatles T shirt with the studs on it.

She pulled out some Tabitha Simmons over the knee boots and changed everything into a MCM mini tote. She topped it with some huge Olive People shades and was ready to go. As she looked in the mirror, she smiled at the bag 'cause Ray Ray and New Jack bought them for her and Tasha and then Jamaica bought Naomi one. That is also the first time she gave Ray Ray some pussy raw. Jazz shudders as she thinks about how nervous she was to finally let him enter her. She knew once he did this raw, he was going to be hooked. This news is gonna blow the girls away. Especially when she tells them that they've been doing it on a regular.

They had all agreed not to go there with sex other than oral 'cause it would change things. Good luck with that! She dipped and it was so good. She just hoped she wasn't the only one. She texted Tasha to see how far away Naomi was and then texted

Ray Ray to tell him that she was about to go to get her hair done. He immediately CashApped her for it but had to be careful 'cause he was in the car with J-Money. He said that Mocha was on her way to Ah-Donis shop too, and be careful. Jazz laughed at this because she knew Mocha, Tasha and Naomi were all in Naomi's Bentley Flying Spur on their way to get her.

Naomi.....

"What the fuck do a bitch want to wear?" Naomi said while listening to Pink Friday and smoking a blunt. What was she going to wear that she can build around her new Louis Vuitton Artsey bag? She finally decided on a denim Gray cat suit that she snagged up at Alexander Wang. Add some gray ankle booties and gray Dior bangles and she was done. She sat on her Rice bed and texted her girls to see how far along they were before she headed out. Jazz was the furthest, way out there in Valley Ranch, so I should go get her last. Mocha stays the closest to me so she will be first. Tasha could be anytime.

She texted a while and said at the last minute that she had to go pick a package up from Krickett. Naomi was so proud at where the girls were right now and the direction they were heading in. The only one that bothered her at times was Mocha, she seems distant from me at times but then I get it where I'm concerned 'cause I'm deeper than the rest besides Jazz.

I serve the boys through my man Magic and I make it happen which is how I was able to cop this Bentley that I'm coming through in. Yeah I got the hood bitch staples, a Benz, a Lac and a 750 BMW, but this Bentley was Jamaica's idea. And I ain't tripping cause we been having so much fun together. It's crazy that this is the same nigga that I vowed to destroy but I must cause Tanesha's life was precious and the lesson must be taught to a bunch of people about life. Naomi takes one more deep breath before she gets up to go get the last part of her outfit and head out the door. Her chrome 357.

Mocha.....

It's like the old saying, "You can take the Ho out the....." and that's what played through my mind when I went inside my closet. I decided to wear these killer Blumarine cream calf boots that lace up in the back. A high-waisted Fendi skirt and cream cashmere turtleneck sweater. A Hermes belt and a huge Fendi logo shopper tote. My Chanel logo earrings and I'm good to go.

You never know who you might run into coming out of Ah-Donis or inside for that matter. Plus I might bump into my secret boo, but his girl be at Ah-Donis so I doubt he will chance it. J-Money texted me a while ago saying that he was going to go eat with his boys and that I should be careful 'cause he heard Ray Ray say Jazz was on her way to Ah-Donis too. While he was at Spud's earlier he paid Ah-Donis for my hair and tipped her. This nigga is full of surprises. I guess his paranoia role is a defense mechanism because it seems now, this nigga does everything in his power to let me know that I'm number one.

The sex is off the chain even if it's just oral sex. One night I got nervous cause we were fucked up and he kept asking to fuck. I told him you know you not ready. I played it off and sobered his ass up real quick with talking about getting pregnant. To shut me up from talking about that he shoved all nine inches back in my mouth and to get over his urge to fuck, he laid me down and fucked my throat like a pussy. He came so much I don't know how I swallowed it all.

I thought he was going to rip my titty off the nut was so intense. That goes back to my old profession. As I sit back and wait on my crew, I laugh at the future knowing that nobody is going to be ready for what we got in store. Nobody...

Tasha..........

Today is all about comfort. Plus, I got some running around to do before and after Ah-Donis. This shit Krickett is sending me is going to send my clients into a coma. So I pulled out a bad ass olive colored leather Balmain military jacket with some Good American camo leggings, a Gucci wife beater and studded Louboutin military boots. I crammed all my stuff into my YSL duffel bag. It's electric blue for my pop or color block appeal. Some big loop earrings and a gold Movado watch. I go all out even down to my fragrance, Marc Jacobs Daisy. That has been my favorite since he came out. I look at myself one more time before I head downstairs with the stuff I am taking with me. One bag is for Ah-Donis shop, one for my girls and one for New Jack and his family.

I feel like since I've been with New Jack I have changed a lot of his ways. After what happened with Bozo I sat him down and told him how he has to switch it up some. Not that I want him to change his personality, just his approach to life. You would never know that he is smart as he is.

He really is far from an average dope boy, but his flashy ways is what keeps him in the game. I'm so sick of his social media alerts, he is like the king of social media. I sometimes wonder how he has time to make as much money as he do. I'm just waiting for the day he interrupts our sex to go update status or like something. But our sex be so off the chain he has no time.

I got to represent for BBW's everywhere. Right? I can't wait to see the ugly looks on these Ho's faces in a few months when the hood is turned upside down over me and my girls. Let me double check all my shit, Jazz just texted and said her and the girls are outside. For some strange reason today felt like it's gonna be a hell of a day at Ah-Donis.

Diva's Revenge

Ah-Donis......

When the girls pulled up in the cocaine white Bentley, they knew heads were going to turn. Out the bay window of Ah-Donis shop they all seen heads turn. Some casually but the hood rats broke their necks to see if it was a baller going to Spud's. When the four of them got out, you could see all the different types of devastation on Ho's faces. When they walked in, the place was full of life. Music is always playing at Ah-Donis. One minute you could be jamming Natalie Cole and the next the newest J. Cole. You never know, but it's always crunk in her shop. Right in the center of it all was Ah-Donis in a black and white Armani dress with the yellow patent leather belt and Kenneth Cole riding boots. Her hair was up in a white girl bun on top of her head and she had on Versace geek glasses.

In her shop it was only her and three other girls that did hair and they all stayed booked. She had a couple girls named Keisha and Destiny that washed and removed hair and basically prepped your hair, but it was only Ah-Donis that touched the girl's hair and that came at a cost to have her that exclusively. I think every beauty shop in the hood across America had a Keisha and Destiny tied to it. The girls quickly said hellos and sat down and started the process of getting braided up for their sew ins. Ah-Donis couldn't wait to grill the girls about the hood gossip.

Diva's Revenge

"So, bitch I know the booster game been good but a Bentley?" Ah-Donis asks Tasha.

"Naw, that's Naomi shit. That nigga Jamaica felt it was time to step her game up." Tasha smiled in admiration to Naomi.

"Girl please that nigga ain't got cheese like that. I know you got to be doing something on the side." Ah-Donis exclaimed.

"I'm just chilling and know this. It's me that put me on point and keep me on point. Jamaica just adds to the pot." Naomi says as she high fived Jazz and Mocha.

"Whatever it's Jazz I should be rubbing up on, she the doctor fucking the baller." Ah-Donis laughs as she blows the heat off the marcels while she spins them.

"Don't do me bitch. I'll prescribe yo ass some shit that'll have you clucking like a chicken." Jazz said while playing on her phone.

Tasha jumps up and grabs Naomi keys and goes to get her stuff for Ah-Donis and one of her girls at her shop. While she was gone Ah-Donis continues to grill the girls about the boys. Other girls also knew the girls and talked to them also. When Tasha walked back in she had an ugly frown on her face. Mocha asked her what was up.

"I think I just saw Cheetah' em pulling in. Don't that bitch still got that money green Lexus truck? If so that was her with Shanky and Rah-Rah. So be ready if them Ho's turn up." Tasha told her girls.

"Be ready my ass, your Ho's not bout to have Champion part 2 up in here. Y'all take y'all ratchet asses outside for that, especially you Naomi. I'm for real. I'm not playing." Ah-Donis yells to them

"Really, I'm chilling, it's them Ho's in their chest because of them nigga's beef but a Ho gonna stay in her place before she get that ass smashed." Naomi says.

Sure, enough the door swung open and in walked the three of them and when they looked and seaw them at Ah-Donis station, a look of disgust came over Cheetah's face. She tried as hard as she could to hold it but she exploded when Ah-Donis say they were next after the girls.

"Girl what kind of ghetto games are you playing. You know we come at the same time every week. So we supposed to wait behind these ratchet Ho's." Cheetah says.

"That's funny, you pull up in an old ass Lexus truck with yesteryear clothes on and we ratchet." Tasha said.

"Precious ain't nobody talking to you, ain't you got an appointment at a buffet to go to? Rah-Rah said.

"That's original. How long did it take you to think of that? Now while we are making appointments, can we set you up to get rid of those stretch marks from yo kids. Also, can we all chip in and get you and yo crew some inches of hair with the first number 2 and not one. You low budget bitches been rocking cheap hair for years talking about you going for natural." Jazz said.

Diva's Revenge

"Yeah, and are you still paying a car note on that old ass truck? I just want to make sure it's insured because you parked next to my Bentley, and I'm scared that you might not be able to afford full coverage insurance in case you bump into my car". Nyomi brags.

"Oh, you mean you and fat Albert made enough money at Old Navy boosting to get a Bentley? Y'all must had freak Ho throw in her pole dancing money and 'miss goody two shoes' worked on enough dogs at the free clinic she works at." Shanky laughs and high fived Rah-Rah and Cheetah.

"Really, you are talking. Ain't you the same bitch begging for me to dress you and yo crew? Y'all out there. Y'all the same Ho's let niggas trap out your Section 8 housing. Y'all lucky a nigga text you back!" says Tasha.

"And bitch I haven't stripped since the last time you were on Maury trying to find yo last baby daddy." Mocha says.

"Whatever, all your Ho's is wannabes. Y'all want what Rah-Rah and Shanky have." Cheetah says.

"What bitch, second place everywhere you go? Your time is up. You go blink and the hood will be gone from under yo feet." Jazz said.

"You could never be what we are in the hood. Everybody knows who run the hood Bozo "Cheetah says to Tasha

"Look bitch it's time we cut all these Shenanigans out and we set the record straight. I am a boss bitch. I run with boss bitches we fuck with boss niggas. The only reason you are even still eating in the hood is because to us, y'all pose no threat. You better wake up and look around. Take a hint from Scooter and Mel. You see how they met they expiration date on some dumb shit? You are thirsty and if you pay attention to a boss, I'll quench yo thirst, but bitch mark my words, you get in my way, like a buffet, you'll be all I can eat, and I won't stop till I'm full. Play stupid if you want to, but bitch go google the word truth. Look around you at the four bitches next to me, that's us. Now get yo nothing ass somewhere and wait on her to do yo synthetic blend hair!" Tasha says.

"Don't nobody wanna hear that shit you is talking about. And mark my words, you go pay for Mel and Scooter. That's my word." Shanky vows.

"Bitch I know this Ho ain't tryna chunk a threat cause you'll be reunited in a few seconds you keep it up." Nyomi says.

"Once again you are talking out of turn ole fake ass Foxy Brown!" Rah-Rah yelled.

"And what?" Nyomi said.

"Bitches pop off!" Jazz said and surprised everyone.

Ah-Donis saw that things were about to go south. She quickly jumped in.

"Tasha, I asked y'all not to do all this up in here. Y'all gonna have to leave if y'all up in here with that. Y'all go have to leave if y'all go do all that. You Rah-Rah!"

"Miss me, you need to tell the stunt double for B.A.P.S. to simmer down before a bitch heat that ass up!" Mocha laughs and speaks.

"You act like you mad!" Cheetahs ask.

"Mad? Tasha bitch I'm mad at y'all clothes. Tasha give these Ho's yo card so they can look like something" Nyomi says.

"All your Ho's are jealous of my crew. If it hadn't been for..."

Before Cheetah could finish what, she was about to say the door flew open and in walked Dior, J-Shun and TT. The whole beauty shop busted out laughing. It was so surreal that seven of the hood's baddest were standing here going at it and in walked the worse of the worse. When Tasha and Dior locked eyes it was instantly a look of disgust.

TT was just chilling. This was Tasha's first time seeing them since she had been back on the scene. The circles that they traveled in was so far from Tasha and her girls that it was rare that they would cross paths at all. Ah-Donis said that they still came through and sold stuff but since she'd been back, everyone had kind of left them alone. J-shun was the first to speak up and when she did, all hell broke loose.

"What's up Tasha y'all?"

"Girl you know we don't do each other but I'm gonna do you one solid. Please stop stalking New Jack on social media. He doesn't need you to like everything he post. We are good, as a matter of fact, we going to go eat after I leave here and then go home together!" Tasha bragged.

"Hey, do you get any Baby Phat or Deveon stuff for sale?" Jazz Asked.

Before Dior' em could answer Jazz made it clear it wasn't for her. She offered it to Cheetah and Rah-Rah and Shanky. As Ah-Donis finished up the girl's hair, they exchanged more words with Dior and J-Shun.

J-shun bragged about these 'ballers' that ben trying to get at her. Finally, no one could take it anymore so Ah-Donis asked. "If all these dudes on you and want to get with you, why y'all still stay together and share that car?"

Everyone laughed. Eventually they left and so did Tasha and the crew. The exchanged icy glares with Rah-Rah and them and all jump in Nyomi's Bentley and left.

Going down the freeway the girls jammed Lil Boosie and texted the boys. Nyomi was busier than the rest, she was texting three instead of one like the rest. The girls each thanked Nyomi for the ride, Tasha for their stuff and departed.

Tasha was last, she and Nyomi talked for a while before New Jack met up with her to go eat and run errands. As Nyomi sat in her car and smoked her blunt, she thought about her next move as well as the girls. She texted Scoop to see what he had for her and from there do some more planning. One thing that she and Tasha concluded about was it's time to turn up the heat.

Diva's Revenge

When she texted Jazz and Mocha, they both agreed. Buckle up, shit was about to get bumpy.

Chapter 12: Collect Calls

I knew shit was going to smoothly for us, Tasha thought as she waited for the operator to put her through to accept this collect call from Krickett. A million thoughts ran through her mind.

Now was not the time to have all these problems. Why was Krickett calling her collect from jail in Austin? A lot is going to happen today and the last thing she needed was bullshit with Krickett. She took a drag of the blunt and waited. But what she heard no blunt could prepare her for.

"Okay, so what's up?" What do you need me to do?" Tasha asked calmly.

"First off, you need to find someone else to bond me out because they are looking for you too. They got me for the damage we did last month at Burberry. But I refuse to fold for these Ho's. But they have set my bond real high. So, meet with Desiree and give her the money. It's a cash bond only." Krickett says all this casually".

Diva's Revenge

Tasha is now nervous cause she did not want any of this on her plate. To add to all this Krickett talked about their running a story about them on the news in Austin and asked for information on her where abouts. This sent Tasha into panic mode!

She asked Krickett to tell her where she kept her money to bond out and how much was the bond? "Girl, I don't have but five grand set aside for that, but my bond is fifty. So just meet up... "Krickett was saying.

"Bitch! I don't have fifty stacks to drop on yo bond. You know I got a mortgage and car notes and all kinds of other bills. Girl you trippin!" Tasha replied.

"Well, who going to come up with yo bond when they get you?" Krickett replied hysterically.

Tasha knew what she meant by that, and it threw Tasha for a loop that Krickett came at her like this. Sure, I have the money, but Krickett is not good at paying her friends back. I have that plus plenty more but it's not something I want to do. But I also respect the rules of the game. Overall, she is my fall partner so I will bail her out. But I'm go let that bitch sit for a day or two so she can think about her mouth. She got me fucked up for real. Now let me get my fat ass up and get ready to go to Jazz house for what's about to go down. I wrap up things with Krickett.

"Look lady, I got you, let me put it all together. Give me a couple of days. You know New Jack be on me, so I have to do it without him knowing".

Right now, I'm about to send you money so you can go to commissary while you there and get some phone minutes to call me. Its $200 and I'll see what's up. I love you and chill I got you. I'll call Desiree and let her know I got you. I know she is lost without you there." Tasha said shaking her head.

Tasha shook her head because she did know her, and she knew this would probably be the last she seen or heard of this fifty thousand dollars. Oh well, part of the game. It will be all coming back soon.

Later at Jazz...

"Okay Naomi, you ready? You are sure that all of them are together? "Jazz asked.

"Yeah! I left it there in the hood and told them I was about to go run errands. Scoop said they still there shotting dice." Nyomi said.

'Okay this is crucial that you sell this right because everything is timed for it. Uncle Mitch is ready and all that so let's go." Jazz says.

The boys all had rode with New Jack in his Range Rover. Scoop had snuck over and hit his taillight and knocked it out.

They waited till right when it got dark to put everything into motion. Nyomi call Jamaica.

"Hey daddy, where are you?" Nyomi asked.

"Still in the hood with my niggas, What's up?"

"Magic just brought me twenty fire of those thangs and I'm not in a good position to move them to you. What to do?"

"Where are you? Well come get them because we go have to meet up and divide it anyway. We can kill two birds."

"Right here by West Dallas. Meet me at that Home Depot"

"Gotcha baby, we on our way now".

New Jack turn to the boys as scoop looks on and tells them that they got some urgent business they need to take care of right now.

They stepped to the side from the dice some to get details and immediately the four of them hump in New Jack Range as night falls. In twenty minutes, they are across town to Nyomi. This is not unusual for her. She plays the role like havening to move big weight make her nervous.

When they pull up on her, she is sitting in her car playing on her phone. Jamaica gets in and kisses her. J-Money come to the window and ask why to get the drop like this? She was already prepared for this and told him that Magic was near me and decided to give me what he had for now.

No big deal. RayRay took charge and him and New Jack started to put the stuff in his truck while Jamaica and anyone talked. Before they left, she warned them to be careful cause Ft. Worth Avenue is hot. As they left, she sent the text to Uncle Mitch.

Five minutes later the boys were on the road and suddenly saw flashing lights behind them. New Jack looked in his rear-view mirror and spoke

"Isn't this a bitch"?

"Niggas be cool, it's probably some minor shit. Just chill. Yo truck straight so what" RayRay says calmly.

As the boys sit there, a thousand thoughts went through they head. As the officer came to the car, all of them clinched. New Jack rolled down the window and asked the officer what's the problem?

"Well, y'all have a taillight that's out on your truck, but since you rolled this window down, I smelled illegal substance". Officer Davis says.

"Davis."

"Well sir, I was inward that my light was and I'm responsible for the illegal substance you smell. I did it earlier but there is none in my truck. If you let me make it, I promise to park my truck till I get this fixed" New Jack pleaded.

"Well sir we have a couple of problems with that. First, I need to search the truck. To make sure it's no more. If I search and it's clean you can go. Don't lie to me if it's something in there, now is the time to tell me" Davis said.

"No sir. you can search"

J-Money kicked New Jack seat. Everyone was shocked at him saying this. They all exited the truck and was searched before they sat on the curb. As the officer searched the truck New Jack whispered to them.

"We hood this nigga haven't even called for backup; we can talk him out of the weed in the truck"

"Nigga we got twenty-five bricks in there! What the fuck you mean ole dumbass dude?" Jamaica screamed.

"Nigga say the shit just a little louder so he can hear you" New Jack said.

J-Money just put his head down in his lap cause him and RayRay knew what was about to happen. Sure, enough the officer came out with the three duffel bags full of stuff.

He places them on the hood of the truck and called for backup.

Within ten minutes another car pulled up. They both talked and pointed and next they walked over and read us our rights before placing handcuffs on us. Next a van to transport us came and within thirty minutes we were all entering the county jail.

One by one the boys went to the pay phone to make their phone calls. This was the moment of truth for all of them this is how they were about to see how down these girls were. One by one the girls got right on top of it all and called Armand to handle it.

The boys waited to go to arrangement to find out the changed and the bond. They all were devastated to find out that they didn't have a bond. None of them. They came back and called the girls. The girls said they would get on top of it. But for now, they would bring them money for commissary. They would all be to visit them tomorrow.

Meanwhile at Jazz...

As the girls each accepted the collect calls, they told Scoop about the progress and kept in touch with Uncle

Mitch. It took a lot of doing to get the judge to no bail them, but Armand was able to do it.

He also kept the amount vague because it would disappear in a couple of hours. Now it was time to apply pressure to the boys. The visited the next day is when the girls change positions of power on the boys, but they didn't even know it they wanted them to have long night to think about everything.

Visitation the next day...

Luckily for them all the boys were put on the same floor so when the girls had Armand call them out the were together. Armand came to let them know that the girls couldn't be seen coming in there under their names cause of what was to happen.

Everyone understood. Especially RayRay. Armand went on to explain that for $175,000 dollars all the dope could disappear to a small amount. They would get a year of probation out of it and all walk away. If they agreed, he would be able to get an emergency bond hearing on the grounds of the number of drugs and have them out in three days tops. It was up to them.

All of them eagerly agreed to pay up. They boys said give them an hour and the money would be to him. All the boys talked about it a little longer and then went back to their tanks and called the girls and told them what to do. By six o'clock that night it was all taken care of. Over the Next few days, they all went to court and bond was set on new lower changes. Armand arranged bond and all the girls there to pick them up. All the boys thanked the girls. They also looked at them in a more serious light now.

They were all happy to be out before Christmas. Armand told them they, court dates were in January, now it was time for the to regroup.

Tasha...

I wasn't expecting Krickett to keep her word, but she did, plus some. No, she didn't give me cash but she out in enough work for me, with Christmas next week, we have a lot of shopping to do. I don't know how her, and this guy name Bo done it, but they got six $32,000 Louis Vuitton signature alligator men's jackets. In brown, black and white.

I gave all the girls one for they man and said sold the other two. We want to Louisville, Kentucky and cleaned up and made things pretty much even.

First time telling me he loves me. Now he gives me the keys to his cars for me to drive and all that I answer his and now he has me in all his social media information. We took about just going away as a group for Christmas.

I suggest Jamaica or Barbados and he agrees. He said for me to book it all and we would surprise everyone at dinner. He told me money was no issues, which was music to my ears.

Mocha...

Dayum it's seems like this trip to jail was like a shot of act right for J-money now it's like I can't get enough of him I don't even have much time for my other boo j-money takes me everywhere with him we are always together doing things now.

I'm around him when he takes care of business and all that he hands me is his phone and tells me to find this and do this for him and often I must talk to whoever because he is driving. Our sex is still the same, only oral. I guess he isn't that gone huh? He really spends money on me and now it's no hesitation at all. I can't wait to see he got in store for Christmas. Now if I can figure out how to see my boo without J-Money being in the way. That's the key. I think I got it figure out; Next trip to Ah-Donis is gon be a little bit longer than normal.

Nyomi...

I'm the hood everyone knows that a bust could spell the end for a nigga. But not in the boy's case. Uncle Mitch gave me all but some of the dope back. A few crumbs to send to the lab to make sure the case sticks, but I have all twenty-five bricks and the plan was to fill them and put back for the girls later. The $175,000 they paid to get out will be spilt like this. Over hundred grand will go to Tanesha's mama.

Armand and Uncle Mitch take fifty, and we spilt twenty-five. We decided to give it all to Tasha for the jackets because we know she took that loot from Krickett. Me and Jamaica sat down and talked to each other in between sex and about how things. Should go. I also ran it all by Scoop,

Magic and the girls. When I talked to Jazz, she told me about RayRay surprise to Jamaica.

I quickly told her no because as of being on bond we could go there. Plus, that requires going through customs and names and that's not good. So, she said she would suggest Hawaii for them. Scoop said that the boys have come out the hustle with a whole new outlook and with Jamaica I can see that. The money didn't hurt them, but they still needed to make it back. So, they had Nyomi double up what they normally get, and they went to work.

Nyomi made sure they got them all. And they blessed her for being a down ass bitch. As she told the girls, money is adding up quick and this will be a nice pay day. It's all about execution.

Chapter 13: Party Over

RayRay...

I let Jazz convince me to go to Hawaii for Christmas and it was well worth it. As we ride together to court this morning. I look at this beautiful strong woman.

Since I was able to get next to her, she has made my life so much better. She thinks and keeps me on point about life. My son loves her and so I do I she held things together when I went to jail, where most lame hos would have fucked up. I mean I know I'm on my way to court for probation but right now looking at her I'm on cloud nine. Armand said we should be in and out. No more than an hour. My boys go to be there too, and we all are getting probation.

A year is nothing considering what we could have got from all we had. As we pull into the parking lot of the courthouse. I see Jamaica and Nyomi and Mocha and J-money. I knew New Jack and Tasha would be late in order to make a scene. I look at jazz hands and see the two-carat ring matching tennis bracelet I got her for Christmas. I got her other stuff too. But she was surprised when we got home to find that New Maserati for her. She almost fainted but deserve it. She is a good girl in love with a thug.

We across the parking lot to J-money and Jamaica and we exchange daps and hugs. Damn that ho Mocha always look read to fuck. That ho makes my dick hard sometimes. Especially her dick sucking lips. Let me shake this off and go in here and take care of our business.

J-Money...

I'm like counting all my blessing that we are not facing some real time because of New Jack dumbass. I mean he still my boy, but I am fucked up at him about this shit. I tried to take my mind off it during Christmas in Hawaii, but It was hard. Me and Mocha had sex everywhere you can think of. Part of me want to fuck her but she might be banking on that. On night though she got close and right when I got ready to stick it in.

I got scared. But I really don't care because I smash this other ho that I been knowing for years. But Mocha oral sex game is so off the chain. I went with RayRay and while he got Jazz a Maserati, I got mocha a new Benz truck. The biggest one they had. I felt it was time for her to get rid of the crown Victoria. She just cried when we got back, we have been having a lot of fun. I admit at first, I didn't trust the bitch but after she held me down when I went to jail, I got mad love for this bitch.

Diva's Revenge

As we sit in the parking lot and wait for the rest of them to show up, she sucked my dick and swallowed all my cum. Right as she gets done this nigga Jamaica walks up to my car as she is raising up. For some strange reason he had a fucked up look on his face. It's probably from seeing my dick. Fuck it I fix my shit and we jump out and talk till RayRay pulled up.

Jamaica...

Hawaii was so much fun. A nigga got see some shit I ain't never seen before that nigga RayRay did his best shit with that me and Nyomi got really close after all the shit with this arrest. But she been showing me the truth in how she approaches business for me. She made me look at shit totally differently now. Overall, it's made me gain so much more respect for her.

To show her that, I bought her some land to start building her own place that I'm go pay for. I also got her four rare Chanel vintage bags. We on our way to court I'm kind od nervous about this year probation because it gets in the way of me getting the fuck out of dodge therefore, I brought her the land for her because I don't plan on being her much longer for this shit. I may try to get it transferred to somewhere else I haven't figured it out yet.

But I know the time is coming I can't talk to her or no one about it because I don't want no one to try to talk me out of it all. Oh well. As we pull up in the courthouse parking lot. I notice J-money ride, so I pull in behind him I jump out to go talk to him about something. When I walk up on the ride, his Bitch Mocha is coming up from giving him head. it caught me off guard to see his manhood and her doing that. I know the nigga brags but to see the act made my face frown. But I brushed it off and went on with what I had to tell him.

New Jack...

After Tasha I don't think I'll ever fuck with a skinny bitch again. We supposed to be on our way to court, but Tasha pulled over on the freeway and is sucking and licking on every part of my body. I have come twice before I must beg her to let me make it her only compromise is why now as we speak, I am sliding down the freeway smoking a blunt and getting head. It's hard to control the wheel cause Tasha got that seizure head for real. We had so much fun trying different shit in Hawaii she even let me bang a Hawaiian bitch while she tossed my salad. A freaky bitch but on point with business. It amazes me how much game Tasha got when it comes to boosting. Her and Krickett are the fool with it.

But because of me, Tasha doesn't have to do as much. For Christmas I spent 100 thousand to redo her whole house for her. I had to do something to match the jacket and Audemar watch she got me. I love that she not greedy and she does her best to bring equal to the table with me she well respected in the hood and although its other hos out there none of them can fuck with what me and Tasha have. I'm proud of her and as I get ready to bust in her mouth for the third time I know why. We quickly exit and when we get into the parking lot, I see my boys all waiting on me with mask on they face. Me and Tasha both laugh as we get out there and join them.

In Court...

Court started at 8:00am. By 9:30 all the boys had been seen and they were all in the parking lot profusely Thanking Armand for his miracle. Armand informed them where to report to on Monday morning. That would be a problem for New Jack and J-Money, neither were early birds. but Armand told them that it was no set time if they it before 5pm. Each was given harsh words by the judge and given one year's deferred probation. Which meant that when they completed it, it would come off the records. That was another small blessing in they favor.

Armand also convinced the DA not to press the issue of suspending New Jack license. The day had gone so well that the boys treated the girls to Cheesecake Factory. Everybody was in good spirits, but they knew a lot depended on who you get as a P.O. because they could make yo life hell. They would wait to see what Monday brings.

Diva's Revenge

RayRay...

I decided to get up while jazz does so by seven we were both walking out the door to head out for the day. I knew it was going to be a little traffic and I did good. I made it there by nine. When I walked in, I was caught off guard at the secretary.

She was so beautiful it's no way that she is from Texas. She looked like a spitting image of Nia Long. But a tad bit thicker she glanced up at me the clipboard to fill out the information and told me to have a seat.

When the bitch got up it was another big surprise, she had ass for days she disappeared for a few moments and then came back and winked at me and showed me to my P.O. office he was cool and on the first day he made me piss for him. He told me to take the cup and told Stephanie to watch me do my thing with the cup. As I stood in the bathroom, she is watching nothing but my dick.

I instantly got that boy on grown man to show her what the business was. Her eyes bucked at the full package and now it was my turn to wink.

As she reached to take the cup out my hand, she passed me some napkins when she gave it to me, she gently rubbed my dick head to get the piss and precum off. I just stood there she left with the cup and went to test it for my P.O. she told them it was clean with a wink. My P.O. told me the next time to come see him, asked about my job and told me what my fees were. Once I left, I immediately texted my boys to let them know that we hit the jackpot with this bitch Stephanie.

Stephanie...

As this ugly ass nigga rocked his shit up, I kept thinking to myself how lame this nigga is. I admit, jazz man did have a huge dick and I couldn't pass up a chance to touch it. Before it's over with, I will have all four of them. I text jazz and let her know he has come by, and it went smooth. She texted back thank you and I sit and wait on the other three to come in. and sure enough each one came. I was told to put the bug on J-money ear that I can help him have clean test in the future so he can pass on the others, so that was my mission is to gain their trust. It wasn't gon be hard. I knew all of them was dirty, but I already had piss to make sure they believe me.

Jamaica...

This nigga RayRay say this chick that work at the P.O. is our inside girl. He swears she bad too. But I know RayRay taste. He lucked up on Jazz for real. When I get there, I see the bitch and I admit she bad for real. We flirt back and forth and then I go meet my P.O. He cools but I can tell her will send a nigga to jail too. He tells me to drop piss for him and Stephanie escorts me to the bathroom. She b ends over and I look down her shirt, she looks up and smiles. I smile too.

Then the bitch grabs my dick through my pants and strokes me, I take it out and piss in the cup. Once I finished, she bends over and cleans me off then she takes me in her mouth once. She raises up and without a word she leaves. My shit comes back clean, and he tells me the rules. I gave him my first set of fees. As I leave, I look back at her once more. She places her finger in her mouth and sucks on it. I nod my head and tap my watch.

Stephanie...

I text Nyomi and give her all the details she texts me back a smiley face. I jokingly tell her I may have to test him out. Like a true playa, she gives me the greenlight. She tells me I know who her man is anyway. Do my thang. So far, he is cuter than what Nyomi said. But I want to wait before u say who's the best looking.

J-Money...

After I left mocha at the Cheddars by the house, I made my way to probation. I still can't believe what RayRay said about this girl name Stephanie that works here. But then Jamaica said the same shit. So, I must see what's up I walked in its empty at the desk, but I hear a female laughing somewhere. So, I decide to sit and play on my phone. suddenly, I hear high heels. I look up and down and damn near drop my phone. These niggas did not give this bitch her props enough she shakes my hand lingers a bit, and then hands me the paperwork to fill out I run through it and hand it back. she takes me to my P.O., and we exchange words about coming earlier. As Stephanie stands behind him and tell me to be quiet.

He shoves a cup to me and tells Stephanie to test me. We go to the bathroom and as I'm pissing, I close my eyes. I feel a hand enclose around my dick, I look up and its Stephine she shakes the pee off and wipes me down. Before I know what's up, she is swallowing my dick. She sucks me till I cum and hops up, take the piss and winks, before she leaves, she tells me that she knows I'm dirty, but she got this one for me.

If me and my boys are interested, she will take care of us. She will schedule us to come in at her time we exchange numbers and I leave as I'm leaving; I bypass new jack. He got Tasha in the car with him. I joke with her for a minute and then I tell new jack about the girl inside he tells he knows.

Stephanie...

I text Mocha and tell her all that happened. he was too much. I could not pass that up. It was better to get at him before the girls destroy them. She texts back a fuck you, I'm gon kill you. As I put my hone back in my purse in comes New Jack and the games began again.

167

Diva's Revenge

New Jack...

I ain't gon lie the bitch is bad but she can't fuck with my big baby. I will play it by ear and see how it goes. I rush through my paperwork and hand it back. My P.O. gave me hell about coming in earlier. He gave Stephanie.

The cup to go test me and we go to the restroom. I can tell she surprised that my shit is so big. I smile to myself. She bends over and takes my dick and rubs it on her lips and breast. When she goes to put it in her mouth, I tell her another time, my gal in the car waiting. She winks and gathers my piss.

She does what she need to do and then my P.O. gives me rules and asked some dumbass questions. I burn off and continue my day. When I get in the car Tasha has a grin on her face as she plays on her phone. For some strange reason I felt that I had been caught red-handed. But I brushed it off.

Stephanie...

I tell Tasha she got lucky she was in the car because he was good as git. She tells me to check my backseat she put my payment in there I thanked her and told her when they next time was.

Jazz...

"Daddy, you know that you love to blow weed. Well at work we got this steroid that we give to cancer patients to help them eat food. But it cleans your system also. I can start sneaking it and giving it to you and the boys. Tell you what when is the next time you report? "Jazz asked.

"Next Thursday mamas. Jazz why are you there for me the way you are?" RayRay ask.

"Because you didn't give up like the average nigga. Now I will give you the shot and then you can let them know if they want it, I got it for you." Jazz says.

"Alright mamas" RayRay replied.

Jazz already had the "shot" ready and was to give it to him and his boys until they finished probation. Once they seen him do it, they would follow him.

Next Week...

Jazz gave RayRay the shot with minimal hesitation. When he left, she texted Stephanie and told her he was on his way. When he got there Stephanie made up a story about the P.O. wanting to test the piss himself.

This made RayRay nervous, but it was all part of the pan of course RayRay passed, and he called the boys and told them what was going on. All of them immediately wanted the "shot" from Jazz. She met them at New Jack house and gave it to them. Jazz texted Stephanie and told her to be expecting them. One by one they all passed. They called and thanked Jazz and RayRay. Now it was a ritual that on the day before reporting they should all get the "shot" from Jazz.

Later the girls met with Scoop and shared all that was going on. He was very pleased. He told them how the boys were acting in the hood like they are Gods. The girls wanted them to continue to feel that way. It was only a matter of time now.

Chapter 14: Death Around the Corner

L ook grimy ass bitches, it's time to pay for me to shut up. I have pics to show all four of y'all men explain what I know to be true. Get yo shit together and be ready to deal in an hour and a half."

Jazz and the girls looked at the text and picture of them together in astonishment. They knew Bozo was going to be a problem, but not this soon. Uncle Mitchel explained to us all what needed to be done but we were still in a daze. How could they be so careless? They worked so hard to put all this together and it was all on the verge of going down the tube over this nigga Bozo. Jazz and Tasha outlook was getting him here and pay whatever he wanted. Nyomi felt that he wasn't going away that simple. Mocha felt that he wasn't going away that easy. Mocha and Uncle Mitch is the ones that came up with their plan. It really all depended on Bozo when he gets here, how things turned out. If he was smart, he would play be the rules. But you never know with Bozo.

"Bozo......"

Ever since Deniece told me about these hos being fake, I can't get this thought out of my head. Why the fuck is these four hos sneaking around meeting up behind RayRay and his boys back. It made no sense. At first, I had the thought that these hos are the Feds but after they killed Scooter and me, it would give been game over. I thought maybe these hos are some professional jackers and going for the big pot. When Deniece told me what she told me before she died, I couldn't believe it.

What she said could destroy these niggas but then I sat back and thought it would mean more to these hos for me to keep quiet and let them do their thing. Plus, when I tell them niggas all they could do is kill them and keep it moving with being on top in the hood. I'm going to make these hos pay me to shut up. It's a lot less hustling for me and Cheetah. Regardless the ball is already rolling so now I'm just gone wait and see what jumps off. While I wait, I'll call Cheetah and let her know what's up.

"Hey boo, what's good on yo end?"

"Shit, fuckin with Jr and Bam, taking them to get some shit for school." Cheetah said.

"Right now, I'm about to go meet up with Jazz and her crew. That bitch Deniece told me about some shit on them hos that you are not gon' believe. They..."

As Cheetah listened, she couldn't help but laugh at him. Deniece ass will say anything to get a hit. It's no way them hos could be up to that type of shit. And I know they hang together because they come to Ah-Donis shop together. I listen to what he says but I blow him off and hurry up and get off the phone to deal with the kids. We say our I love you and we gone.

45 minutes later.......

"I knew your hos would come to yo senses because you know I hold all the cards" Bozo said to Jazz.

"Come in before people see you coming in here!" Tasha yells.

Nyomi is quiet sitting on the bed at the room in dark shades. In her mind she would just smoke him and deal with it all later. Mocha and Uncle Mitchel seem to think they get it. Bozo looks around the room and takes all the girls in before he sighs and starts his speech.

"You all almost had me fooled. At first, when Deniece told me I thought y'all were jackers or the Feds but then when she gave ne the second part, I started to watch y'all to see what shake. Y'all are good, them niggas will never out it together, that y'all are working together against them. But why? That is what's been eating me up. Now I want to know this, and it will determine how we proceed. Do y'all want to keep me quiet and include me or just shut me up and have me go away?" Bozo asked them.

"Nigga this is not a debate. Tell us what the fuck you want and depending on what you say, we will let you know if we agree." Nyomi spoke.

"See the problem with you bitches is y'all don't know y'all place. But after today, you will. Trust me. Bozo exclaimed.

"That's funny cause the only bitch in the room is you. Your right, after today a bitch will know her place!" Mocha stood up and spoke.

"I think all that swinging upside down went to yo brain. You need to sit down and wait on the next tip to come." Bozo returned.

"I've never stripped but you do wish you had before long." Micha said.

"Look I'm tired of dealing with you Ghetto Twins. Can I talk to the hos with the money? I need a half a mill to go away with what I know, period." Bozo dead panned.

"Done! Meet us back here in an hour flat." Tasha spat.

A smirk comes across Jazz face and Bozo asked what for.

"All you worth is half a mil. It's funny not even six months ago you were king of the hood, now you are selling secrets. Sad. I think Bozo the clown is to nice for you. It's more like crusty." With that she walked up to him and spat in his face. Before he could react Tasha and Nyomi had guns in his face.

"Get yo bitch ass out of her before I accidentally on purpose dump on you. Be back in an hour flat." Tasha said.

Diva's Revenge

Nyomi winked at him, and Mocha slapped him on his ass and said "Good Game" before he left. The girls called Uncle Mitch and told him it's a green light on him.

10 minutes later up the block....

Bozo could not believe his luck. Not only did these bitches humiliate him but in this rearview mirror he sees a cop running his plates. He thought real quick if he had anything in his car that would get him locked up and then he relaxed a bit. Before long the cop lights came on. He pulled over to a spot off the main road. The cop exited and he realized it was the same cop from the shit at Champion Lounge.

A sigh of relief washed over him because he knew he could talk his way out of whatever. As the cop approached, he noticed that shit was not right. This coo had his gun out. He came up on my car and told me to turn it off, throw the keys out and out my hands in the air. Things didn't feel right cause this nigga kicked my keys in the gutter.

I thought maybe it was an accident do I waited to see what was next. He opens my car door with the gun still on me and tells me to get out. When I do this nigga places me on the ground. I'm pissed cause this is expensive ass Calvin Klein and Versace. But I try to stay calm.

Diva's Revenge

The nigga place hand cuffs on me without even telling me why. He lifts me up and places me in the backseat of his car. He then searches me entire car. All the shit he takes he put in a Ziploc bag. Once, he's done, he gets in the car. I ask what's up. "Well son, you fucked with the wrong muthafucka and today is not yo day." Uncle Mitch says. He hits the radio and Tupac song "I see death around the corner" came on.

He smiled at me through his sunglasses, and we took off. We drove all the way to the south to a seedy ass motel. Once we got there, he pulls up next to a car that I'd seen around the hood.

What I see next takes my breath away. The door opens and Mocha steps out smiling at me. All I can do is pray.

Inside the room......

The cop shoves Bozo gun the bed and suddenly Mocha yells for some bitch name Rumpshaker to come out. Mocha introduces all to each other. Uncle Mitch speaks next an explains how thigs are going to go. "Okay Bozo, today you are going to learn a valuable lesson about life. See Miss Rump shaker right here? She is the police secret weapon. Why? Because we get her to of niggas like you and make it look good. She has killed seven dudes for us and never did any jail time other than for prostitution. Now today you will make a number eight but unlike the others you have a choice of how you die. One of three ways, one is the dumb way, when I take the cuffs off you can try to fight for your life and she will work you over with the very sharp switch blade she has. Two, is she can give you a fatal hit of dope and you OD on her? Nice and clean but embarrassing. Three, I can shoot you up with thus insulin and let her suck your dick to death literally. Now those are your three options but there is one that I and Mocha here would love. We can take the cuffs off, shoot you, I say you tried to flee when I busted you and Rumpshaker. Rumpshakers write a statement to match, and you go down in shame. Either way it's the end of the road for you pimpin. So how you decide is on you. I'm about to cock this pistol and give it to Mocha, take these cuffs off and see how smart you are," Uncle Mitch says.

When Uncle Mitch removed the cuffs, Bozo sat and looked around the room for a long moment. He asked one question "So there is no way out of this but death? No amount of money?"

Uncle Mitch shook his head no and before they knew it Bozo lunged at Rumpshaker, and true to his word, Rumpshaker cut Boz so many times till it was unreal. As he lay there on the floor, Mocha left the room quickly. Rumpshaker took her nails and racked them across Boz face for good measure. Uncle Mitch left and went up the street and waited for the dispatcher to call on someone to respond.

When it finally come over the radio he rushed to the scene and secured it. As he was securing the scene, he watched as Scoop walked away from the Bozo car. He shot Uncle Mitch a pistol and salute and left. Bozo thought that was his key kicked in the gutter. It was the key to the rental scoop used and set on fire after getting in Bozo car and coming to the room. Scoop walked to Mocha car, and they sped away. Uncle Mitch told them both to find something to do for an hour.

Uncle Mitch and Rumpshaker were right out of Hollywood. He debated whether to leak his name or let them discover it later. As he thought about it he decided later would be better. He called the girls and let them know it was over. They took a statement from Rumpshaker and the crime scene people took the samples under her nails. Uncle Mitch offered to give her a ride downtown to get away from the scene. They played as Bozo tried to make her given him sex for drugs. She said no and the fight happened. Resulting in Rumpshaker cutting him fatally. No further investigation needed.

The Next Day at Cheetahs....

"See bitch this is the shit I thought we got past. Why the fuck is Bozo not answering his texts. And his ass stayed out al night. See this type of shit that makes me feel nothing about fucking around on him." Cheetah says to Shanky in her living room.

"Girl I would give anything to have my baby back taking me through shit." Shanky says.

"Oh, girl I'm sorry. I'm just glad you start back talking to me. Rah-Rah still on some. More shit. Girl he called me yesterday in some lame ass story and now I know it was game to pull this stunt. He go pay for....."

Cheetah paused as her phone rung. It's not a number she recognized so she put in on speaker phone.

"Hello!"

"Is this Chelsea Wilson?"

"Yes, this is her. Who's calling?"

"I'm officer Gilmore with Dallas Police Department, we found a black Lexus registered to you at the scene of a crime. Would you so happen to know Ebony Williams?" the officer asked Cheetah.

"Yes. Why?"

"Well yesterday around 8pm he was involved in an altercation with a female prostitute, and it resulted...."

Cheetah could not believe what she heard next. As the tears streamed down her face, she just looked at Shanky who shook her head too in disbelief. After a few moments of silence, the officer asked if she was still there. She planned to go identify the body. He told her they would hold the car for a few days to process it for evidence but afterwards she could have it. She was stunned beyond words. How could this happen? That's not Bozo to fuck around with the streetwalkers. He feared catching something and bringing it home to me.

Bozo is a big nigga, how was this prostitute about to kill him? Something just is not right about all of this. It is too much of a strong coincidence that he goes to meet these hos and come up dead. Bozo would normally text me to let me know his next move. Maybe RayRay and em' got him on out they to officially take over the hood. One thing is for sure, I'm not Rah-Rah and Shanky, I'm go die for mine and make whoever responsible gon' down in the process. Shit about to get ugly in the hood and they not gon like the Chetetah they about to see fasho.

The Funeral......

Everybody in the hood knew Bozo or knew of him, so of course you know his funeral was going to be packed to capacity. Cheetah has both of his boys by her, and his family sat at the front of the church. She was held by Shanky and his mama. As she cries, she kept her eye on everyone that walked past his casket. One by one they all filed by. She damn near lost her mind when she seen Jazz and RayRay walk up to the casket, followed by the rest of their crew.

Diva's Revenge

Before anyone could know what to expect Cheetah jumped up and went towards the group of them. She yelled at the top of her lungs.

"I dare your grimy ass bitches to show yo' faces up in here. If I had a gun, I would put one in all y'all faces. I know y'all is behind Ebon dying. You know it and when I'm done the whole hood gon know it. The hood will never be yours. You spineless bitches ain't got what it takes to last one week. Ebon kept all of y'all alive!" Shanky pulled her away and some people asked Jazz and them to leave.

As they were leaving, they locked eyes once more with Cheetah. Once, they got to the cars the boys all asked the same question. No one understood where Cheetah was coming from. Everyone thought that Bozo caught it with the prostitute. Jazz explained that during mourning, you often blame the death on other parties to ease the loss. It even gets to the point where some people start to blame themselves. They all said a few words to each other and parted ways. They all agreed to meet up later.

When they all got in their cars suddenly, shots rang out and before you knew it, New Jack windows in his car were shattered. Everyone quickly got out the way and fled the scene when they all got up the street, hey looked in their rearview mirror and seen a running Rah-Rah holding a chopper.

They rode to their destination in complete silence. All RayRay said to everyone is one simple thing. If Rah-Rah or any of them get in our way, we gon' run through them like an eighteen-wheeler. No more games. We are the king of the jungle now, everyone else now becomes either a part of the pact or prey. Let's eat!

Chapter 15: Almost time

As everything seemed to settle down, all the girls were about ready to take the boys out for the final count. Jazz had been giving them the "shots" every week and Stephanie had been testing them with a clean repot. Each of the boys often complained about a mild case of diarrhea and nausea but they gladly accepted them over jail time. They even felt that they were losing weight. To compensate for this, Tasha got them a size smaller than normal. All these things appeared to the guys as odd. By Jazz being a doctor, she explained it away as some of the side effects, but it was nothing major.

The boys continued to make money as now the hood was truly theirs. They are making almost three times what they were at first and Magic is having trouble keeping up. But he loved it! No one really saw Shanky, Rah Rah, or Cheetah around the hood but Scoop. You know he sees everything. They still give Bozo and Scooter and Mel shout outs in the club, but no one is really messed up about the loss. Typical hoof shit. Each of the girls and Scoop, Stephanie, and Mitch all go inti overdrive. They all feel that the end is near.

Each one of them go about doing their part in preparation of the takedown. It's strange to each of them how this journey lasted ten years and is now almost over. The tricky part was each of them doing their final parts without being noticed. But they manage...

Uncle Mitch

For the past six months, I have been working my ass off to keep these girls in the clear while they do their thang. At times was unsure they had it in them but between them and Scoop, they have really surprised me. As the lead on all the cases involving them, I had to get rid of certain evidence in order to make it all go away. But part of the plan was to keep it all hidden to be revealed in due time.

Everyone is shaping up to get the job done and it makes me proud that'll be able to give mama closure and something to live off of for the rest of her life. It kills me that it took ten years to bring it all to her, cause in that time I watched a beautiful spirit become so bitter and corrupt. The hood changed her for the worse, I also feel bad for Bozo and Scooter and Melly Mel. They were caught in a war they knew nothing about. But in time, I hope they can smile down from heaven at the revenge we about to serve.

Diva's Revenge

Stephanie......

My girls didn't have to do much convince me to help them get even with these ugly mofos. I mean me and Tanesha go way back. She was cool people, and I had a lot of respect for her. She taught me early never to settle for less and show to use my sex appeal to get what I wanted. But from her death it made me change and I got a job. Of course, it would be a job that allows me to do what I love but it's a job, nonetheless.

It's really a challenge to mess with RayRay, he is so damn ugly, but he blessed with a huge dick. I enjoy sucking it but I can't stand him because this nigga really think his game is on point. Not! Now New Jack has become the one I look forward to. Why? Because he is a freak, and I can relax when I freak with him.

He lets me suck on him the way I want to, and he talks to me while I eat that dick up. His cum is always thick and he is always ready for round 2. To me J-Money is the cutest out of all then and his sex is boring and to the point I feel he does it to get a clean report on his piss but I enjoy sucking it cause he got that young nigga dick that gets rock hard and has a lot of veins on it! Jamaica is the one that precums a lot and that I truly have the most fun with.

He fucks me in my ass because I explain that I have a man and with his big dick, he would know someone been in there. But Jamaica never gives a fuck. He even begs me to let him hit it bare.

He claims it has more feeling. I expressed to him that I don't roll like that. He got to be out of his mind if he thought I would let him bust in me. Yea right! I play with myself all the time thinking about the one time that I sucked New Jack while Jamacia fucked me. It was off the chain, and I got it on video.

The girls were tickled pink seeing their men acting an ass with me. I like Nyomi, she was so play about it, so was Tasha, even gave me tips on what he likes. It was Mocha who looked fucked up at what went on. I can't place my finger on I but she not right, she always seem to have a hidden agenda. Or maybe it's just a fellow prostitute intuition. I hate that thing are about to end but I'm glad they are getting their payback. R.I.P Tanesha Duvall.

Nyomi...

Its crunch time and now well are about to show these niggas why we are in their life. Things have been going smoothly but I can't shake this fucked up feeling that I am missing something important. In preparation or the showdown, I have already stashed up 50 keys of cocaine, so me and the girls will be okay. But I will get the boys for another large amount when the day comes. I have been peeping Magic for the big drop. I had to convince that he could front it all to them and it was all coming back. No worries. As the time gets closer, I am spending more time with my Boo and Magic.

Diva's Revenge

I'm going through the motions of emotionally cutting myself off from Jamacia. I'm doing little stuff like picking crazy fights to get room for us to plan. I blame it all on my period and he loves me so much, he okay with it. If he only knew. I have started to go to their stash house and secretly move all the money and guns to our stash house. Nothing to obvious. But in its place, I am putting counterfeit money until the day comes so not to alarm them.

I have been meeting up with Armand to take care of the cars. He surprised me with what he came up for us. Ever since this nigga been on Jazz shot, it has killed sex for us. I mean I still do the oral sex for him, but I don't know. I guess it's the face I hate him so much and now he is fucking Stephanie. He does too much but it's all good and makes me do what I do to him even more easy.

I really ain't seen those bitches Shanky and Cheetah and Rah-Rah. Ah-Donis say they still come and get their hair done but we never cross paths. I think them hos got the message. But they beef is with RayRay and then which Is all good to me. We don't need no more distractions in our way while we take care of business. I can't wait to see Mama Vi when she gets the news.

Mocha...

I am so ready for this to be over with. I'm ready to go off and start my new life with my Boo. This has taken up ten long years of my life. And at times I'm not even sure I wanted it as bad as my girls. But I wanted it for Mama Vi. I made sure we look out for her in the end. For some strange reason here lately, it seems like I am out the loop on what's going on but when I ask they all say that we waiting on Armand and Uncle Mitch to tie up lose ends. At first, I was kind of mad that they were letting Stephanie in our business. I used to work the cuts with her, and I know how shady she can be but maybe it's because she reminds me a lot of myself. But she expressed her l of Tanesha and I understood.

J-Money has been cool, but he seems to be letting all his new money go to his head. I mean he still spoils me rotten. But now he got this cockiness and arrogance about him that wasn't there before. It's like now that they are top of the food chain, they, well really him and New Jack, think they shit don't stink. He has started to get flashy like New Jack. Even RayRay spoke on it. Our sex is okay but a part of me wishes for him to make love to me. This is the part if the game, I can't reveal to the girls. I feel J-Money and really don't want this to end but I really don't want him as much as I want my boo! In time all things must end, and new things begin. It's just a matter of how they will end.

Jazz....

I'm not gon lie I'm kind of nervous yo be moving out of Texas, starting over is such a big thing especially in a new city.

But I am comforted with knowing my girls will be there with me. I am glad that the end if thins ten-year ordeal is over so I can get back to my real life of dating, and enjoying my career, and lastly life in general. For the past weeks I have been talking RayRay that I must go to a series of conferences in New York. Not true! The first times were the interviews for hospitals up there. I have the job.

Now I am meeting with realtors and finding lofts for all of us to move into. With the money we have now, I was able to buy lofts for all of us in Sotto. With all that we have and stand to walk away with, we should be good. All the lofts cost a little over two million altogether. We all sold our homes in Texas. I used a catalog of the realtors to find buyers. I couldn't use Kim Jones because she would have blabbed to RayRay and New Jack because she knows both.

Nyomi and Tasha wanted three bedrooms because they love space. I got a two and so did Mocha. RayRay recently bought me new furniture and so I will use that until we I find some more. We all decided to give Mama Vi I stayed in downtown plus $250,000 and a car. At first, I was nervous about Shanky and Rah-Rah, especially after she shot at us but now them and Cheetah seemed to have faded from the planet.

Which is good cause I would hate to add them to the list. Nyomi estimates that on top of the 50 keys we have now, she says we will have another 100n to flip up there. She knows a couple of people so that's her thing, I will be too busy with work. Tasha is planning to work lightly and date more. I don't know about Mocha; she is always so closed lipped about her plans. No matter what, I love my girls and I'm happy that we all will still be together.

Tasha...

This is a bunch of hard work. I am having to take pictures of all these niggas clothes and show them to these three consignment stores. All of them are more than eager to buy it all cause it's all in good shape. When the time comes, I will sell it all to them and what they don't want, give it away. It's so much shit between the four of them. I have been saving up all my extra money like my girls have. I am so excited to be moving from Texas. I feel if I stay here Krickett and her greed is going to be my demise. We will be set up enough, so I won't' have to hustle right away.

New Jack really started to grow on me, and I really had doubts about us doing them in but when Stephanie showed me the video, it showed me how heartless a nigga really is. I mean we are heartless too, but I guess it's different. Cause I don't mess with no one else. I just wish Cheetah and her girls made better choices. Who knows? In the aftermath her and the other thirsty bitches can help these niggas get back on top. I doubt it cause after we done; they are going to be finished. I don't think it will be any recovery. I think I may take a year or two and go to school for fashion and out all this to use. Who knows?

Scoop...

As I stand here in the mirror and I wash my mask off my face, I smile. I played the game of chess and now it's about to be check mate. Game over. I haven't decided if I want to take my Boo with me when this is all over with. I love her and she has been down with me from the beginning. When I started to plot 8 years ago on how to get these niggas back, I never knew it could be done. I just felt I wasn't an angry nigga mad and humiliated by some nothings. As these four dudes beat my ass over a lie and knocked out my teeth, I grew to hate all five of them.

The four that did this to me and the leader that rowed them up. So, when I watch them burn my Toyota Camry that I had worked hard for and looked at my teeth on the ground, I set my mind to get them all back. They all used to call me Camry because of my car, but my name then and my name now is MAGIC, short for Magnificent. My mother knows when she gave birth to me that I was something majestic and names me accordingly.

Yes, these lame ass dudes have all been working for me. The same niggas you beat up and ran away from the block Jamaica is tasting me on a regular cause I make sure Nyomi head, and I fuck her in the hood ask Scoop. When people see her around me, no one ever pays it any mind.

None of the girls. Cause I'm just Scoop. But I made it my business to know their every move, to better crush them. Just my luck that I cut into the girls, and they were on the same page. Now it's time for us to destroy them. All of them. I have saved up a little over two million dollars. I don't get a chance to spend it because I've been busy playing Scoop. But it's time for these niggas to meet the real boss.

After all this is over, I will probably leave with my Boo. She and I make a good team and we could have a lot in Florida or Philly. We shall see. I've been watching these bicthes Shanky and Rah-Rah and they seem to be on to the next, but this grimy bitch Cheetah, she is the one to watch. I remember getting head from her back in the day in the same Camry when she and Bozo first got together. If she could see me now. If all of them could see me now. Like I said game time is over. Check mate.

Diva's Revenge

Later...

As the four girls exit their doctor's office none of them paid much attention to the Dodge Charger parked down the block. Cheetah knew of the doctor's office, but it made no sense to her. Jazz worked across time at Tri-City. So why were they all here? She planned to find out. She made her way into the doctor's office and casually went up to the sign in sheet. What her eyes saw she could not believe. So what Bozo was saying was true. This means he died at the hands of them and not RayRay them. She had to let the world know what she discovered. She hurriedly gathered her thoughts as the receptionist asked if she could help her. Before the lady knew it, Cheetah was out the door.

She grabbed her cell phone and texted Shanky to tell her where she was. Shanky texted back she was at home, so Cheetah said stay by the phone, give her two minutes to get in the car and she was going to call her, it was urgent.

Cheetah got in the car and started it. She was so excited about what she knew. She finally was going to be able to crush Tasha and her crew and now for sure she could get J-Money. As she dialed Shanky, she went to put it on speaker phone. As she is about to talk to her a beep comes that its someone on the other line. Cheetah screams in the phone to Shanky "Bitch you are not gon' believe what I found out. Don't go anywhere, let me answer this other line!"

In Cheetah excitement, she clicked over and dropped the phone as she approached the light. All in a matter of seconds, as she tried to bend over and get the phone off the floorboard her foot accidentally hit the accelerator and Cheetah car sped up and went straight through the light that was red and her car careened into two cars and was fish tailed out of control. As the car smashed against both cars and the telephone pole, Cheetah was smashed in the car.

Later that week...

"So, what y'all mean to tell me she was pregnant with twins when she died?" Shanky is beyond words as she listens to the report on her only true friend. At this point Shanky don't know what to do. In a matter of six months, the game had completely wiped out all that she knew. In a matter of no time, she went from being in V.I.P to being on W.I.C. RSVP to AFDC and it scared her. All she could do is cry as she thought about how now was, she going to survive.

Cheetah didn't really have no family like that, and Bozo family really don't fuck with her outside the kids, so how was she gon pay for her funeral. Something to give soon. This is too much. As Shanky held up the phone from the county coroner, she went to look in on her kids one last time for the night. As she looked at them, she whispered to herself and asked "How could yo daddy leave me here with a broken heart? He supposed to protect us."

As tears rolled down Shanky face, she walked to their bed and kissed them. She then went in the living room and prayed after she prayed, she smoked a whole blunt. She threw the roach in the ashtray and picked up the 3.57 Scooter gave her, placed it to her temple and pulled the trigger to end it all.

Diva's Revenge

Chapter 16: Too close for comfort

This is the last time Jazz went to New York, it was decided she kept her return off by a day. This way they could all meet up with Scoop and Uncle Mitch without interruptions. So, they decided to meet at Jazz real house in case RayRay decided he wanted to drop by her town house to do something, at this point they couldn't afford any surprises. This was also everyone chance to get a last-minute update on everything. Since no one wanted to be bothered, they all turned their phones off once Uncle Mitch arrived.

He started the meeting off with saying he had bad news. When the girls left the clinic earlier that day, when they left from eating at Chipotle, that real bad accident that had all the ladies blocked on Preston was Cheetah. It stunned everyone. He also told us that in the same week Shanky ended her life by suicide. She blew her own brains out while her kids were in the other room asleep. This took everybody breath away for real. For a spell, there was nothing but silence as everyone took time to regroup.

It made each of them reflect in how precious life it and how petty their beef was with the girls. This made them hate RayRay and his boys even more. Because of them, yet another family is damaged.

Because of that one coward Jamaica, it has ended so many lives. After a while, it was Nyomi who spoke first.

"Magic, baby, are we still on deck for the hundred from you? I done convince them to pay half upfront and the rest as they make it! We still gon' come out ahead, right?"

Magic had a real cavalier attitude about it when he said yes. As I the girls were wasting his time or something. Nyomi chalked it up t frustration and not being able to spend as much time as he wanted to with her. But with him playing Scoop and her playing her role, it was hard.

Tasha was next with her update, and it was green lights with the three consignment stores. The night before everything kicked off, she would clear it all out with Magic and Jazz. Nyomi would have them tied up with the drop and that would give Jazz and Tasha to pack all four boys up.

Jazz said that the realtor found buyers for the girls and boys places. All of them came out to a little under the five million, which meant that the girls would only have to kick out five hundred for the lofts in New York. Armand was going over the papers as they speak and would deliver them tomorrow for everyone to sign and finalize. He also was able to find buyers for all eight of the boys and the girls seven too! Minus the one for Mama Vi. By them living in New York they all agreed they would do subways and taxis until they all figured out if they wanted to buy new cars.

Next, they talked about the shots. It was decided to reveal it to them anyway as Jazz showed them the other news. Nyomi reported that she had replaced all the money from the stash house with the fake. Armand had given Uncle Mitch all of their official new identification to match the paperwork on the stuff in New York. Only a few minor changes have been made. They finished the meeting agreeing that in three days it was all going to take place. Nyomi once again ran down her part.

Uncle Mitch heard it all he decided it was time to go to Mama Vi and let her know everything. She would be there when it was all said and done, so he needed to her to prepare for it all. Arrange for her things to be moved to Jazz town house and all of that. He knew it was going to be a lot for her to grasp son he needed time to talk to her through it all. Next to leave was Tasha. She told Jazz to walk to her car with her because she had stuff Jazz wanted from the internet. As Jazz complained about how tired she was and ready to go to bed because she had an early day coming, Tasha remembered that she had stuff for Nyomi and Mocha too.

When she went back in he came around the corner to see Nyomi and Magic all hugged up. Before Tasha could say a word, she noticed Mocha off the side licking her lips behind Nyomi back at Magic. At first Tasha thought it was a dream but then Magic blew a kiss and winked at Mocha. Mocha held up her hand in a cell phone motion and mouthed the words "Call me daddy." To him. He said back "ok". Stunned into disbelief, Tasha backed out of the house and hurried down the driveway. She had such a crazy look on her face that Jazz couldn't help but ask what's up.

"Bitch you act like you seen a ghost." Jazz joked.

"Maybe so, Bitch I need to get home, I know my mind playing tricks on me." Tasha said.

"Why you say that?"

"I just saw Magic and Mocha wink and blow kisses at each other."

"Yea girl, you tired, Mocha wouldn't do that to Nyomi."

"You right girl, I'm tripping."

"Yea you are, go home and call me when you make it Diva."

Jazz shook her head at Tasha and walked back in. Mocha wouldn't dare do that to us. We to tight and come too far to go there. We better than that, that shit is for them other chicks. We major bitches. Besides, Mocha knows you share recipes not men. When she walked back in her house, she found the three of them in her den, she hated that Tasha told her that cause it made her look at Mocha differently. And Magic too. And it made her feel guilty for possibly keeping a secret from Nyomi. If it's meant to be, it will come to light. It always does.

Diva's Revenge

Next day...

Mocha kept texting Tasha to get the stuff she said that she had for her, but she wasn't answering. That's weird. That's not like Tasha not to answer, so Mocha texted Jazz to see what's up. She texted back that she was busy and would talk to me later. Nyomi said she was busy too. Oh well, she texted her Boo to see what he was up to.

Across town...

Armand had been having a nagging feeling about something for weeks. He ran into one of Mitch's sisters in the store one day, this was a sister who was a black sheep in the family. She was the one that stayed in the hood while Jazz mom and Mitch moved to Cedar Hill. She kept saying how she wished her son would get his life together and be something like his Uncle Mitch.

Armand asked how old he and she was said he was twenty-four. She explained that Mitch and Jazz mama hadn't spoken or seen her or her son in over ten years. She is a single mom and works all the time to provide for her son. She didn't know where she went wrong. She asked me had Mitch ever mentioned her and I stayed face and said yes. He did but not how she would have liked.

After the conversation Armand could not get the coincidence out of his head. He went and looked at the boy's information once more and then at Jazz. It was no way. On a hunch he called New Jack and asked him to call his mama and ask for his sister's name. After twenty minutes Armand heart dropped when New Jack stated the name of Jazz mother.

He had been trying to reach Mitch to tell him. He was amazed how Mitch missed the connection and now see the resemblance. He had to let them know before it was too late. Tomorrow everything is going down and he had to let Mitch know that that was his nephew. Armand just hoped it wasn't too late.

Nyomi...

As Nyomi sat and smoked a blunt in her car, tears rolled down her face and what she was about to do. All of it was now sinking in on her and overwhelming her. It hurt because he had grown to really be her Boo. Even though she knew going in that none of this was for keeps, she still grew close. It hurt to now see that it all was coming to an end after 10 years. All for Tanesha her heart hurt to lose a friend but now she knows that's a part of the game. As she started her car one last time, she drove away from the house she knew to be home after tonight she knew that it was truly over. She closed her eyes to shed the last tear and inhale the last drag of the blunt. She out on Lil Kim "Stay that Bitch!" and rolled off to out the finish touches on the plan.

Chapter 17: The Birthday Bash

L ike clockwork, everything fell into place. She met the boys and got the money for the hundred keys that they were getting from magic. Jazz claimed to have worked late for the night, so they made an excuse for her.

Tasha lied and said she on her way out of town with Krickett, but both was at Nyomi house waiting for word from her with Mocha. Uncle Mitch hadn't been answering his phone, but he knew what time the big birthday party was going on. He was going to pick Mama Vi up for it all. Stephanie was coming also. Mocha was tied up with some last-minute thing, but she said that she would be on time.

Tasha and Jazz went over it all in their heads and on the phone to Mocha and Nyomi. The girls kept calling the boys to see if they were coming together. RayRay told Jazz he was about to go get all of them to meet up with Nyomi for the big drop. Staying in their roles the girls told them to be careful.

Across town....

Uncle Mitch went to the storage to show the evidence to the boys and put the nail in the coffin. After the way him and the girls planned to crush them, he had no worries that they would all stay silent, but you never know. He called Mama Vi and told her about the time he would come and get her and afterwards he switched off his phone. Everyone he needed to talk to, he was see in a short while he hoped everything went smoothly cause if not, he was going to act an ass.

Nyomi...

So, the plan was to call them and let them know to come and pick up the one hundred keys but when they get home, the party is going to start. It's going to truly be a birthday bash because it is going to be a surprise for sure.

Mocha...

It seems so crazy that we are at the end. I mean as I walk through this party supply store and get all the things Tasha and Nyomi told me to get, it seems surreal. I know that tonight is going to shock everyone in so many ways. Let me go and go hurry and pick up this cake before the bakery closes.

Jazz...

Tasha and I are rushing to get it all taken care of. The movers have cleared out all of stuff out of all the houses that we wanted gone. In a couple of them, we left furniture as part of the deal. Now I must head to the spot for the party. I grab the envelope to give to each of the boys at the party. She couldn't do nothing but smile at finally being done with all of this and being able to move on with life. With the five envelopes, she left the house with Tasha looking back for the last time.

SHOWTIME...

Nyomi made the call to the boys when everyone was there, and the place was decorated with the party favors. She placed the cake on the table and all the girls, and the rest looked at it and got all choked up. Everyone patted Mama Vi on her back. She had to be strong, but it was going to be okay after tonight.

The girls, Uncle Mitch, Magic, and Mama Vi, and Stephanie all waited real patient. It was decided that Jazz and Tasha and Uncle Mitch would be the ones with the guns. It was Mocha and Magic jobs to keep watch for outside movement.

Diva's Revenge

When the knock came at the door and Mocha looked out and seen it was all four boys, Mama Vi, Stephanie, Uncle Mitch and Magic all went in the back room until the signal from Tasha. When Nyomi opened the door, the boys walked in, a bug surprise. Tasha and Jazz pointed the choppas at them at the same time then all the girls yelled "Surprise" and Nyomi was the first to speak.

"Look, don't do anything stupid and you will live to see tomorrow. At this point I could care less but we worked too hard for this day so let's get the party started." with this she grabbed a tub at Jazz walked up with party hats. All the boys' faces were mixed with stunned and anger. Nyomi instructed them that they were to empty their pockets into the tub, strip down to boxers and put on the party hats.

"Bitch you better enjoy this cause all of you hos are dead after tonight" Jamaica said.

"That make two of us then huh. Shut up pussy, you are the reason for this party. Tasha snapped back.

"Man, what is all this about Jazz? Let me know what's going on" RayRay pleaded.

"In due time. And let's quit using names. This is a birthday party to celebrate the birthday of four new lives. Buckle up niggas. "Jazz responded.

"So it was all a game u fat bitch? I should have never blessed you with this dick. I knew better than to fuck a fat ho! Now look where it got me, getting robbed." New Jack said.

"Robbery is the lease of your worries. And for the record, I did you a favor, I made you relevant to the hood." Tasha retorted.

"Look this is too much, get the fuck out your shit and let's get this shit over with before I body you right now." Jazz screamed while pointing the gun.

"So yo college bitch is gangsta now? So, what's up with yo Mocha, I see you are the one without a gun and a voice. Baby did these grimy bitches get you. I'll kill each of them for you." J-Money says. With one fluid motion, Mocha walked up to J-Money and with blunt force, punched him right in the face. When he fell, she spit on him?

"Well, I guess that answers your question Mr. Paranoid. Now get the fuck up, get in yo chairs and let's start the party." Nyomi said.

The boys all went to the chairs and sat down. As if on cue, Mama Vi, Magic, Stephanie and Uncle Mitch came into the room. Uncle Mitch told Stephanie to pick up the cake. She did and together they walked over to the boys and one by one let them see the cake. When each of them seen the picture of Tanesha on it, with her birth and death date and see Mama Vi, it all started to sink in. Jamaica was the last to see it and when he turned to look at everyone else, he knew. Uncle Mitch took the lead and started things.

"I know your niggas is wondering why all of this. It's a statement to the hood of what would never be tolerated. This is eleven years in the making."

As he says this Jazz walks over and gives the boys four of the five envelopes she bought with her. She gave the last one to Nyomi and told them not to open them until given permission.

Next Tasha spoke up.

"Before we go any further, I feel that it is only right that each of us go around the room and tell you who we are. Today the old you died and the new you is being introduced to the world, so you must know who is now a part of your life an why. We will start simple, and they move on to the complex as time goes on. First we will start with Stephanie."

"Hello boys, I know a lot of you think you know me, but you don't. I was best friends with Tanesha, Brian Taylor, and we shared so much together. In was also born a man and me and Tanesha went through our process together. But because of this coward Jamaica, her life was taken permanently. He was a coward because he knew and loved Tanesha for who she was. Plain and simple. I used to talk to her on the phone about him. He met her with me but he doesn't remember.

Diva's Revenge

We were both prostitutes in the gay area. So, when Uncle Mitch and Mama Vi told me what happened, of course I made it in my business to help. You guys never passed a single UA test, I used the girls pee to get y'all through, but my part was something bigger. I just want y'all to know that you have this coward Jamacia to blame for your new lives. Enjoy." Stephanie said.

Mama Vi. She could not look at the boys in the face because it still hurt but she found the strength to say her peace.

"For eleven years, I have sat in my house and hates all of you for doing what you done. I play back in my mind the day I met y'all at the grocery store. I play back why would you take my sons life. I couldn't figure it out for eleven years my friend Mitch has promised me that your day will come. But I never believed it, I just grew more and more bitter. I gave up but these people in this room didn't. And before tonight is over you will know why; all life is precious and what Tanesha meant to them.

Today is a birth for a new life for all of us in this room, but for Brian too. I hope you learn from this. You deserve it you weak ass bitch. My son was a woman to his heart. He was more man than all of you put together. If I had my choice, I would have put a bullet in all you bitches head 10 years ago, but I don't and after to seeing what these people put together for you, I'm glad I didn't. Happy Birthday!" she sat down and for the first time, she looked Jamaica in the eyes.

Next up was Uncle Mitch. He went into the other room and grabbed the bag. When he came back, he handed his gun to Nyomi.

"I know y'all know of me but now it's time to find out why I'm here. First, your niggas are lucky I didn't let Mama Vi and others kill you but after tonight you gon wish I had. Tanesha was close to me cause when I use to go to the gay club, Tanesha Duvall would be there performing a lot. When I found out who her mother was, we became close. I see Tanesha mature to a beautiful woman. So beautiful that she got you Jamaica. I see you over to her house several times I even saw y'all come out the red door motel before.

But all that changed when you decided to be a coward and not keep it real with your boys. Now all of you must pay for it. I was only so much of a force, but these ladies were a beast at getting y'all. I'm here to make sure after they tell y'all how they did it and what they did, that you leave them alone. Each of you after tonight can be facing murder charges. In this bag I have evidence to place you on the scene for Melly Mel and Scooter murders, also for Deniece and Fancy. No, we were never able to prove that you sick bastards killed Tanesha but in this bag is enough to put all of you away." Uncle Mitch said.

'Ain't this a bitch, this fag got down on us? What the fuck? "J-Money asked.

"Oh, that's just the tip. We set y'all up to get busted that day. We set yo connect to take that fall for you to start dealing with Nyomi. The $175,000 that you paid, $100,000 has been given to Mama Vi. As we speak, I have Rump shaker making the video statement that you four guys paid her to kill Bozo, if you come near anyone in this room, it will become critical in your trials. Nothing is what you think it is and after tonight you and this hood would know never to underestimate a homosexual. Or a human being period.

"Well, if y'all so mad about this shit Tanesha why not take this shit out on Jamaica? Why all of us?" New Jack asked.

"Because all of you are bitches and cowards and he told RayRay and RayRay let all of y'all kill someone innocent. So now as a crew, you gon pay." Jazz stated.

"What the fuck you are talking about, I didn't know this nigga was in the punk game. I thought he really didn't know!" RayRay screamed.

"Oh, trust me, before tonight is over, you gon know, he knew. Ain't that right Jamaica?" Tasha says.

"Look there is no need to play every man for themselves. Y'all are all starting from scratch as of now." Nyomi demands.

Next Tasha got up and walked around them. First, she laughed. Then she proceeded to drop her bombs "Well it's time for school. This course is called life.

Diva's Revenge

Pay attention niggas cause its some real shit about to be said. Let me introduce myself, you already know me and my four sisters. See when we were coming up, we were not who you see today. We were always around Tanesha learning the ins and outs on how to be a woman.

My name is Joshua White and yes, I lived on the same block as y'all. I was the chubby little boy y'all always thought was funny. Close ya mouth New Jack you could have never guessed it in a million years. I know you're wondering how we were able to keep this hidden. That was with the help of Armand, your lawyer, who is Uncle Mitch's lover.

All that you thought you signed over was fake, after you left Armand signed it all over to the real us. All that you had was gone as of 6 this evening. All your clothes have been sold and given away to a gay homeless shelter.

The profits of those sales will go to Mama Vi to move Tanesha to a more expensive burial plot that they can share. You no longer have any cars, as all of them except the one y'all came in, is gone. The one you are in have already been given to Mama Vi to get around in.

All your houses and the secret spots you had New Jack has been sold and we made a little over 1.5 million for it all. We used that to buy us all lofts in another city with a new life. We sold all your furniture as well and sold all our homes. Like we told you today is the birth of new life for all of you. We will destroy all your phones and all that after we leave.

"So, you bitches think we gon let y'all walk up out of here, the hood with..." New Jack says.

Just as he was walking the door busted open, and all eyes go to Armand who comes in breathing hard. New Jack jumps up and goes for Tasha and Nyomi sees him out the corner of their eye and loads his body with several bullets. As his body falls to the flow Armand yells.

"No, you can't do that, that's Jazz cousin! Mitch I been calling your phone to tell you that his real name is Keldrick David. He is your sister's child that y'all said was the black sheep of the family. You haven't been answering your phone." Armand pleads.

"What do you mean he is my cousin? I never knew I had family still in the hood. Is this true Uncle Mitch?" Jazz asked.

"I never put two and two together Jazz. I never even seen these boy's real name. Armand took care of all that." Uncle Mitch stated.

Silence fell over the room as all the people in the room saw the lifeless body on the floor. Then in turn, everyone looked at each other than at the other. It was Mocha who broke the silence.

"Fuck it, he was gon die anyway, right? Let's finish and get this shit over with, I got shit to do!"

"Speaking of, let's move on. Ok, it's like this. In each one of y'all laps is a few things. One is a DVD with all y'all having sex with each of the girls here. As we speak, we have some crackheads walking around the hood giving those away.

There is also a DVD of Tanesha and Jamaica having sex, so you know after watching it that yes, he knew she was a man. Just like he knows Nyomi is one. But she will get to that in a minute, my name is not Jazmine Omega. Omega will be true for y'all cause after I tell y'all what I done; you will feel like it's the end. My name is Raymond Davis. I was the one who left the hood and moved to Cedar Hill after Tanesha was killed because my parents knew I was gay.

RayRay also known as Raydrian Jones, I went to school with your brother Corey and with your three goons here, J-Money aka Jakobi Malone, Jamaica aka Millicent Robinson, and New Jack aka Keldrick Davis. But I wanted to have something in life, so I went to med school and it taught me a lot. And I will share with you what it taught me.

Do you know why those shots gave you the side effects it did? It's because those weren't shots to clear your pee, each shot I gave y'all was a different dose of HIV blood from the hospital I work at. In those folders are a recent copy of your recent HIV status. All of, you are positive. That makes five people in this room that are, maybe six, but we will get to that later. I felt that killing each of you bitches would be an easy way out. You took a precious person life; she no longer can live life. So, I wanted y'all to walk around for the rest of your life in this hood as a dead person. To

214

know what a loss feels like. Y'all are nothing now all because of a punk bitch that couldn't face the music."

Jazz looked at Jamaica before she continued.

"All the time that I was with you RayRay, I kept searching for good in you to spare you from this but each of you showed me that you deserve what you got. With the seven million we got from all your stashes and stash houses we will be good for the rest of our lives. Oh don't worry the money at the stash house been gone, Nyomi had been for weeks replacing it with fake money. She also had some other tricks for you but that's all later. Jazz said.

Jazz looked at Mocha as she got up to go in front of the boys, with sudden anger she slapped the shit out of each dude in turn. She kicked and punched J-Money and Jamaica. She gained her composure, and she started her words to them.

"My name is Ramone Washington. I am not a stripper, but I am a prostitute. I am the one who introduced everyone to Tanesha. We both walked the same cuts before she died. None of y'all but RayRay know me, I am a year younger than him, but I jumped off the porch early cause my mom couldn't accept me. I really don't have much to say other than thank y'all for all you've given me. Happy Birthday!"

Mocha smiled at them and then she smiled at Magic. He smiled back and this bought a laugh from Tasha and Nyomi. Jazz was kind of puzzled. Magic got up to take the floor. Today he was in Marc Jacobs from head to toe. He had on no shades so they could get a look at his face. He smiled at each one.

"I know your niggas are wondering who I am? I am your maker. I am the reason your niggas have been eating through my bitch Nyomi. But let's go back farther so I can rally make you familiar with who I am.

About eight years ago, this bitch ass nigga RayRay had lied to you and told y'all that I owed him some money and drew a gun on him, never ever happened. I am the driver of that Camry that you burned. I am the nigga who teeth y'all kicked out. But here is the real shocker. I am Scoop. Yea that's right." Magic relished in this moment.

Each of the dud faces registered surprise at what they were hearing.

"Yea nigga I seen everything and for years I watched your every move and I fed it all to these girls to take you down. I convinced them to team up with me to get at y'all and it worked. I am now 17 million dollars richer because of y'all. I supplied Nyomi and then she gave it to y'all, and I came to the hood to watch y'all work. I supply a lot of niggas in the city, and I will walk away very rich with my true bitch. My money."

At that moment Mocha stood up and walked on the side of him. She then turned his face and kissed him and turned and looked at the group.

"See after tonight me and Magic will be 24 million dollars richer. With the seven I stole from your dumb hos. Y'all can have those lofts, me and Magic are moving to Miami, ain't that right daddy?" Mocha asked. Mocha turns to look at Magic and he delivers another bomb.

"Nawl baby, this is the end for me and you. If you that grimy to do yo girls like this, what would you do to me, I'm leaving by myself now, this is it." Magic went to open the front door and Mocha tried to plea to him. When he opened the door and jerked away from Mocha, he was met by a bullet to the face that blew half the back of his head off and splatted blood in Mocha's face. She stood there in shock at the site when she turned around it was once again Nyomi and Tasha that was smiling.

"So, what's now? Y'all gon kill me too?" Mocha asked.

"No hunny, after we tell you all that we got to say, you will kill yourself" Nyomi said.

She then turned to the door and told Romeo to come in and close the door quickly. She walked over and kissed him deeply and he took his place next to the girls.

Nyomi walked over and with the butt of her gun hit Mocha in the face.

"It's bitches like you that make it so hard. I am always prepared because I'm a boss bitch and me, Jazz and Tasha are boss bitches. It hurt me that you would even betray me and when Romeo first told me what he seems, I didn't want to believe it.

When Tasha reconfirmed it, I went into action you share a lot of things in common with these four niggas. Yea you a man but you are the fifth person with HIV in this room. You been having it though. Jazzy give her, her envelope." Nyomi said to Jazz.

Jazz walked over with disgust in her eyes and gave it to Mocha, she refused to accept it, so Jazz dropped it on the floor I front of her. Nyomi proceeded.

"Ok so my name is not Nyomi King but its Marcus Scott. My mama is big Peggy that had all the dope in the south. She never let me come out much because she knew what I was going to be. But all my life I have stayed in the hood. Never left. All the money y'all thought y'all made from hustling us now back where it belongs. Jamaica you could have been a good nigga, but you have no backbone. Really all that needed to be said to y'all has been. It's about me and Mocha right now. We knew something wasn't right with you. Magic fucked up when he gave me your favorite perfume. We knew your grimy ass was going to pull this that's why you haven't been on none of the planning.

News flash, Romeo has already removed all the money that you and Magic stole. We have twenty-four million. You have nothing bitch. We never bought you a loft, we bought three in New York for us. You were never a factor. All your clothes were sold with these niggas shit. You will be starting a new life first like them because we put out a special DVD with all your real information in it on the internet on your social media site. The part of the money you would have got, is now being divided with Stephanie, Uncle Mitch and Armand. Now we must cut this part short, but we must go. We have a flight to catch. Oh, and Magic was never my man. I have been in love with Romeo from the jump. Romeo tells them why you were involved. "

Nyomi grabbed his hand.

"Well, I wanted revenge because it was my sister New Jack made have an abortion at 16 and then he dumped her, and she committed suicide because she was in love with him. He probably doesn't even remember, but I do, and I'll never forget. Nor has my family."

Part of me wants the bullet through you but like Nyomi and her girls made sure of, y'all already did. Happy Birthday Bitch"

With that Romeo knocked New Jack out everyone looked around the room each other one last time. While Uncle Mitch kept the gun on the boys and Mocha, all the girls went and hugged Mama Vi and all of them cried. It was a long overdue embrace that let Mama Vi know it was time to move on. They were letting her know that the hurt is over. Armand went to Uncle Mitch side and hugged him. As they looked at the boys, they seen the first one crack in, J-Money. He began to cry. Stephanie stood there for a moment and then decided to deliver some sage advice to Mocha that she had been wanting to say.

"Girl I use to see you on the block and always ask Tanesha why she hung with you? You were always so cutthroat, you cut into three girls that would die for you and loom how you repay them. Now you have HIV and it's not the end of the world for you. It could be worse. But go somewhere and start over.

I will help you with a ticket to wherever you're going but that's it. Life is not a hustle or next big come up. You must know your limits. Remember this in all you do kid, pray that your neighbors respect you, trouble neglects you, angels protect you and hopefully heaven accepts you."

With that Stephanie walked off leaving a crying Mocha. As the girl were about to leave the boys all made feeble attempts to get at them but it was J-Money who made the most impact.

"Man, it's like this. I always try to protect myself from any harm and I surrounded myself with niggas that I came to think would protect me like I protected them, but I was wrong. The shit that has been exposed to me today just opened my eyes to how evil this world really is. To you Mama Vi....."

"Nigga, I know your pussy ass is not trying to make amends and shit. It was you who swung on Tanesha first!" Jamaica said.

As that broke out in a fight amongst each other the girls all walked out with Mama Vi, Stephanie, Armand, Uncle Mitch and Romeo. They all stepped over Magic body on the way out the door. As Mama Vi walked to her new Benz. Each of them removed the latex glove that Jazz and Uncle Mitch insisted they wear. They all said goodbyes to the group and all three got in the car and left.

Diva's Revenge

Epilogue

Uncle Mitch...

He went about making sure that no trouble came to those involved. He was even promoted to Lt at the department. Him and Armand got married in a small intimate ceremony in Fiji with close friends and family. With the money the girls gone him, he and Armand had a home built from the ground and are now looking to adopt two kids.

Mama Vi...

After all that happened, she couldn't stay in Texas any longer. She sold the townhouse and Benz and moved to a small town in Louisiana. She keeps in touch with the girls and Uncle Mitch.

Diva's Revenge

Stephanie...

She went ahead and had the full sex change. She moved to Vegas and works as a probation officer. She is in a serious relationship with the owner of a production company. He knows about her transformation and is okay with it.

RayRay and The Boys...

Became the outsiders in the hood. No one would talk to them. Jamaica could not take it, he confessed to Melly Mel and Scooter murders and signed for life in prison to get away. RayRay gave himself a lethal shot of cocaine and took his life. No one has seen or heard from New Jack. J-Money no longer goes by that. He has given his life to Christ and now is a speaker to youth about life.

Mocha...

She was killed trying to rob a trick on the cuts in Atlanta. Her body stayed in the morgue for two weeks before Stephanie found out and came and claimed it. She told the girls and they wired her the money to cremate her.

Diva's Revenge

Tasha...

Is in school and dating. She has opened her own clothing boutique and sells couture clothes. She also helped Krickett get rid of clothes through her store. She is known all through New York for her style and store. She has a blog that is very popular.

Jazz...

Is currently involved with a man that is her type. She is serious. She works at a hospital not far from her loft.

She chills with her man and girls. She lives a real quiet life. She gets her energy from hearing from Tasha all of her escapades that she encounters she is thinking of a full sex change.

Nyomi and Romeo...

They live together and have a beautiful life. She and Romeo are known in the dope game cause of the 100 plus keys they came to New York with. At first Tasha and Jazz tried to talk to her out of it but they realized it the hood in her. Romeo moved in with her and they are happy. He expressed to her that he does want to marry her. So, they are now planning. She also has been talking to the girls about opening a restaurant or club after Tanesha. Who knows what the future holds?

www.ingramcontent.com/pod-product-compliance
Lightning Source LLC
Chambersburg PA
CBHW071838020726
47502CB00004B/1411